P9-DGW-641

Finding Papa

Books by
Laura Leonard

Saving Damaris
Finding Papa

FINDING PAPA
Laura Leonard

A JEAN KARL BOOK

Atheneum 1991 New York
Maxwell Macmillan Canada   *Toronto*
Maxwell Macmillan International
New York   Oxford   Singapore   Sydney

Atheneum
Macmillan Publishing Company
866 Third Avenue
New York, NY 10022

Maxwell Macmillan Canada, Inc.
1200 Eglinton Avenue East
Suite 200
Don Mills, Ontario M3C 3N1

Macmillan Publishing Company is part of the
Maxwell Communication Group of Companies.

First edition

Printed in the United States of America
1   2   3   4   5   6   7   8   9   10
Designed by Kimberly M. Hauck

Library of Congress Cataloging-in-Publication Data

Leonard, Laura.
Finding Papa / Laura Leonard.
p.   cm.
"A Jean Karl book."
Summary: In 1905 twelve-year-old Abby and her older brother and
sister take the train to California to be with their father.
ISBN 0-689-31526-0
[1. Family life—Fiction.   2. Railroads—Trains—Fiction.
3. Adventure and adventures—Fiction.]   I. Title.
PZ7.L5485F1   1991
[Fic]—dc20   90-23742

For Jim

ONE

JUNE 1905

The day had finally come!

I could hardly believe it. Papa *had* sent for us, for Damaris and me and our brother, Joel. We were going to California.

The morning sun shone hot and bright, and the wind was blowing something fierce. I could smell the grass and wild roses in the Smith Kenyons' yard. Off in the distance a freight train whistled on the curve coming into town.

"Scared, Abby?" said Mrs. Smith Kenyon as she stirred up the breakfast pancakes.

"Spitless!" I said.

In truth, I was really more excited than scared, even though we actually didn't know Papa very well. And we surely didn't know this Mrs. MacKay he was intending to marry. But I hadn't ever gone even as far as Kansas City, and here we were going clear across the country almost two thousand miles to California. I might worry a lot, but I liked adventure too.

"So it's all worked out for the best," said Mrs. Smith Kenyon.

"Yes."

Well, it *had* worked out. But I couldn't be sure yet it was for the best.

I had stayed with the Smith Kenyons all that week before the train left because, well, it's a long story. . . .

Uncle George, who had taken us in when Mama died, couldn't keep us any longer when he lost his business and got evicted from his house. He and Aunt Eunice were going to move in with her folks in Illinois. And that's why we, Damaris and Joel and I, had to go out to Papa.

Whether he really wanted us or not.

We hadn't lived with Papa, because Papa had never been a settled sort of man, though Aunt Eunice said maybe that had changed now that he was getting married again.

I squashed down a little twinge of anxiety. I wasn't exactly sure if I was going to like having a stepmother. I didn't know if I would even like Papa. He had never been around enough for me to get to know him.

At school Mary Margaret Vincent (who is Most Aggravating) kept saying, "I do pity you, Abby, having a stepmother."

She also said she expected Papa didn't really want us or he would have sent for us sooner, and asked if we were sure he'd even remember to meet us in San Francisco.

And then, when I wrote my composition about Papa for a class assignment and Miss Johnson read it out loud to the *whole class*, Mary Margaret said, "How could you possibly remember him saving your life when you were only two years old?"

"Joel told me," I said.

What Joel actually said was, "Pa yanked you out of the lake by the hair on your head, or you'd be down there yet with the fish nibbling your toes."

That sounded Utterly Horrid, so I changed it a bit when I copied it down in my Idea Book (which I am keeping now instead of a diary). Everything in a diary ought to be true, but in an Idea Book I can put in my drawings and made-up stories and true things too. Saving my life was one of the few true things I knew about Papa and me.

"I expect your little friends will miss you," Mrs. Smith Kenyon said as she flipped a pancake. "I know my six will."

I wasn't so sure of that. I'd taken care of the little Smith Kenyons a lot, but they were leaping and hollering around, not paying a scrap of attention to me, so I didn't think they would. Dolly Raymond probably would. Dolly was my best friend in the world. I knew I was going to miss her dreadfully.

Mrs. Smith Kenyon said I was such a big help with the children I was welcome to stay as long as I liked, which was very kind of her, I'm sure, but I was glad I only had to stay a week.

Mrs. Smith Kenyon is a very kind lady but not a very good cook. We had liver and brussels sprouts for dinner one night because Mr. Smith Kenyon liked them, and kidneys and something she called carrot potpie another. I tried to eat everything to be polite, but it was a Terrible Trial.

My breakfast pancakes were sitting in my stomach like a lump of dough when the folks came by to collect me to go to the station.

I was all dressed. Mrs. Smith Kenyon wasn't.

She was still in her nightgown and wrapper with her hair up in kid curlers, and the kids were still running around in their underwear.

I would have been Purely Mortified to be caught in my nightgown, but Mrs. Smith Kenyon just laughed and said, "My, you are the early birds, Eunice! You go right along, Abby. We'll be down directly. The kiddies would never forgive me if we didn't get down in time to bid you *au revoir!*"

When we got to the station, there was not one living soul besides us there, except for the ticket seller.

"Better five minutes too early than five minutes too late," said Aunt Eunice.

We all sat down on the station benches, except Joel. He can't sit still for more than five minutes. I don't think he knows what to do with his legs when he's just sitting. Joel has streaky blond hair like Papa's. He had plastered it down with water, but he was so excited he kept running his fingers through it, and it had mostly dried out and was curling up in back at the neck and around his ears.

Damaris looked perfectly calm and collected except for a little tic in her cheek. I guess she wasn't as calm as she looked, or she wouldn't have had that tic.

Damaris is seventeen and beautiful and almost made a terrible mistake and married Mr. Karl Buttchenbacher, who is old and rich. Everybody thought that was a good idea, even Papa—everybody except Joel and me. We thought it was an Awful Idea and that Mr. Buttchenbacher was a Real Skunk. A triple-dyed one with a white stripe about two miles wide running up his backside under his B.V.D.'s.

Damaris finally decided Joel and I were right and gave back her big ugly engagement ring; but Mr. Buttchenbacher got even. (Mary Margaret said he would.) He bought the house out from under us, hauled off the furniture (which he had also bought), and evicted us. That was how come we ended up parceled out to neighbors and church ladies all over town the last week.

But at least Damaris had been Saved from an Awful Fate, and now we were on our way to California. At last!

A few other early-bird travelers began to drift in. Finally we heard the train whistle way far off, blowing for the curve out on the edge of town. Aunt Eunice fidgeted, got up, and looked anxiously up and down the platform.

"I wonder where the Bentons are," she said.

"They'll be here, Eunice," Uncle George said.

Mrs. Benton was supposed to look after us on the train. Damaris had just turned seventeen. Joel was almost fifteen, and I was going to be thirteen on the Fourth of July. We thought we were plenty old enough to take care of our own selves on the train. After all, if Damaris was old enough to marry Mr. Buttchenbacher, she should be old enough to look after us (if we needed looking after).

Aunt Eunice had other ideas. She didn't rest until she found a lady to keep an eye on us all the way to California. This Mrs. Benton had been in town visiting her sister and was about to go back to her home in Berkeley, California, on our train. Aunt Eunice was tremendously pleased.

She said, "I told her how good you were with children, Abigail. You can make yourself useful on the train helping with hers."

"How many does she have?" I asked with a sigh, wishing for once Aunt Eunice hadn't taken a notion to compliment me.

"Three. Two girls and a boy."

Three couldn't be any worse than the six Smith Kenyons, I thought. I didn't have anything to say about it anyway.

Mrs. Benton had come and inspected me and pronounced herself satisfied, and Aunt Eunice had inspected her and pronounced herself satisfied, and that was that.

I did wonder, though, what would happen when Mrs. Benton asked about Papa. Would Aunt Eunice call Papa the Original Rolling Stone or a Born Gypsy like she usually does? Or would she remark that the "mining fever" had caught him when he was young, or that he hardly ever came home . . . even when Mama was so sick?

No. Instead she said, "John's led quite an adventurous life. George and I are glad he's settled down enough to make a home for the children. We do wonder, though. . . ."

"Wonder?"

"This Mrs. MacKay is a businesswoman. She and John became acquainted when he went to work for her. It is an unusual situation."

"Indeed," said Mrs. Benton. "It's difficult for a man to take direction from a woman."

"Especially someone like John, who has been such a . . . such a Free Spirit."

Free Spirit did sound better than what she usually called Papa.

The Bentons still hadn't appeared when the train pulled into the station, its engine clanging and banging, and slowed to a stop beside the platform.

The locomotive vented steam with an awful hiss, and I was almost afraid to walk by, but of course I had to. I looked at the wheels out of the corner of my eye.

"Big, aren't they?" Joel said. Joel knows all about trains, or likes to think he does.

"Enormous!" They were as tall as or taller than I was.

"This really is an old teakettle," Joel said. "Wish it was one of those new ones that go sixty miles an hour."

"Mercy!" said Aunt Eunice. "Sixty miles an hour! It can't be safe for a body to go such speed!"

Joel started to open his mouth, probably to tell her about engines and such. Mama used to say, "Joel was born infatuated with grease." But before he could say anything, the station attendant began calling out destinations.

Aunt Eunice fluttered around, looking this way and that for the Bentons and asking us if we had everything, our socks and shoes and toothbrushes and tickets.

"If they had much more, they couldn't stagger on board," Uncle George said.

It did seem like our luggage was swelling up and multiplying.

Uncle George lifted the lunch basket Aunt Eunice fixed for us and said, "You didn't have to pack the store, Eunice. They aren't going by mule train. If they run out, they can eat at a station café or buy something off the sandwich butcher."

"Well, there's no sense spending if they don't have to. No telling what they'll need cash money for before they set foot in San Francisco!"

"Don't fuss, Eunice. They're going to be just fine."

We were very fond of Uncle George. He was always saying we were going to do fine or first-rate and that we were a credit to Papa and Mama. That meant we had to practically turn ourselves inside out not to disappoint him.

Before we boarded, Dolly Raymond and the Smith Kenyons came trooping up to say good-bye. And, of all people, Mary Margaret Vincent!

Mary Margaret kissed me on the cheek and said she would miss me! Then she said she was sorry we hadn't been better friends!

I almost fell over in a Dead Faint. Had Mary Margaret changed? Could a leopard change its spots? Not likely!

And then she flapped her eyelashes at Joel, and I thought, Aha! Joel is why she came down to the station.

I do not have charitable thoughts about Mary Margaret. I suppose that is a horrible Character Flaw, and the Recording Angel is writing it down with a big black mark against me. Sigh.

Aunt Eunice was still fussing and fuming about the Bentons as we climbed up the train steps.

"We'll be all right anyway, Aunt Eunice," I said, thinking—hoping—the Bentons would miss the train.

They didn't.

At practically the last minute they hurried onto the platform down at the far end of the train.

The train whistle hooted, bells rang, and the engine belched great puffs of steam.

Aunt Eunice called up to us for about the thousandth time not to talk to strangers.

"Yes, ma'am," we said, though I didn't know how we could be expected to manage that, as almost everybody we could possibly meet would be a stranger. Even Papa was practically a stranger.

The train lurched forward as we settled into our seats, and so did my stomach.

Joel looked at me as the train picked up speed and said, "You're not going to throw up, are you, Abby?"

"No," I said.

When I was little, I was always getting sick to my stomach. Of course, Joel would remember that. So does Damaris, but she's not always reminding me.

Damaris unpinned her hat, put it on the shelf over our heads, then looked thoughtful and a little sad as we passed Mr. Buttchenbacher's house out on the edge of town. I wondered if she was feeling bad about not getting married, but she said she wasn't, not at all.

She did look pale, though, and there were little beads of perspiration on her forehead and upper lip. I figured it was the heat making her pale. Or those corsets she has to wear now she's so grown-up.

Maybe if I stay skinny, I won't ever have to wear corsets, though Aunt Eunice says she expects that since I am almost thirteen, even I will be blossoming soon.

Blossoming is what Aunt Eunice calls it when you get bosoms and hips, which are a terrible nuisance, as that is when you have to start wearing corsets to hold everything in and carry smelling salts, because when the stays are pulled so tight your ribs stick into your backbone, you're apt to faint.

Aunt Eunice says once you get used to corsets, you feel like part of you is missing when you don't wear them. I think your bones must go to jelly and can't hold themselves together anymore.

My mind went skittering around from one thing to another. From corsets to how Damaris got saved from making a horrible mistake and marrying old Horse Teeth Buttchenbacher.

But mostly I was thinking about Papa. And Mrs. MacKay. And how everything was bound to be all right now that we were on our way. I hoped we would like Mrs. MacKay. And that she would like us.

It was plain silly and borrowing trouble, as Aunt Eunice would say, to wonder if Papa might forget to meet us. But it was true that he wasn't used to thinking about us very much. For example, he never remembered my birthday, even though it is on the Fourth of July.

There was a long lonesome whistle as we rounded

a curve. I wondered if everyone in Estes, Kansas, heard it and thought about us going so far away.

Maybe, I thought, it would be years before we got back. Maybe we wouldn't ever see Aunt Eunice and Uncle George or Dolly or the Smith Kenyons ever again. . . .

I missed them all already. I even missed Mary Margaret Vincent!

The door from the vestibule at the end of the car opened, and a passenger came through. He stopped and spit a stream of tobacco juice into the brass spittoon at the end of the aisle.

Suddenly I didn't feel so good.

"You're turning green, Abby," Joel said.

At exactly that same identical minute I realized there was something important I didn't know.

"Where is it?" I whispered to Damaris.

"Where's what?" she said.

"The washroom!" I said desperately.

"Next car," said Joel.

I didn't stop to ask how he knew, but made directly for the door.

Once outside our car, I stood there on the metal plate above the coupling between the cars, afraid to move. The wind rushed by while the train racketed along the tracks.

I gripped the rail and watched the ground whiz by. The coach door opened behind me, and a handsome silver-haired gentleman smelling of whiskey, cigars, and bay rum crowded onto the platform beside me.

"Allow me, miss," he said, pulling open the door to the next car.

I didn't say thank you.

I didn't say anything.

I held my hand over my mouth, scrambled across the metal plate through the door, and hoped I'd find the washroom. Fast.

TWO

I made it in time. Just.

It would have been embarrassing to get sick in front of the silver-haired gentleman, but at least he was a stranger. It would have been Horribly Embarrassing if it had been somebody we knew!

When I felt a little better, I read the sign over the commode. The words went right along with the clickety-clack of the train wheels on the rails.

PASSENGERS WILL PLEASE REFRAIN
FROM FLUSHING TOILETS WHILE THE TRAIN
IS STANDING IN THE STATION.

What, I wondered sickily (that's not a word, but that's how I felt), was that sign for?

Then I knew.

Everything drains from the train right out onto the tracks. *Everything.*

Ugh!

I discovered later that the porter comes through

and locks the doors to the washrooms when we're in towns—just in case somebody can't read the signs, I guess.

Travel is certainly *very* educational!

The Bentons had found us by the time I got back to my seat. The porter was stowing their luggage in an overhead rack and a lunch basket and hatbox on an empty seat.

Mrs. Benton had a firm hold on the leather harness attached to her little boy, and the two little girls had gone to investigate the watercooler at the end of the car.

"Abby, dear," she said, "Damaris tells me you aren't feeling well. I do hope you're not going to be ill."

"No, ma'am," I said, though I still felt a little queasy. There was something peculiar about Mrs. Benton's appearance. I stole a glance at her. It was her hat. It looked like a squashed mushroom.

The two little girls came trotting back from the watercooler, catching hold of the chair backs as the train lurched and rattled along. The smaller one was a giggler. The giggles bubbled out of her with every jerk and rattle of the train.

"This is Abby," Mrs. Benton said, and the two little girls nodded politely. "Philippa is eight and Rose is six." (Rose was the giggler.)

"And"—Mrs. Benton smiled down at her little boy—"this is our Buster. He's going on three. Say hello to Abby, dear."

Buster wriggled out of her grasp and jumped up and down on the seat.

"Babby," he said cheerfully.

"Do sit down, dear." Mrs. Benton gave a yank to the harness and Buster slid down with a thump.

Our car was only half-full. It was a chair car. That meant we would be sleeping in our chairs. They weren't chairs actually, but benches covered with red plush. The red was turning brown, it was so old.

Buster examined his seat with interest.

"Hole," he said, digging a finger into the plush.

"Dear me, yes!" Mrs. Benton said. "It is a hole. Aren't you a clever boy."

I wasn't sure about Buster being a clever boy, but Mrs. Benton was a regal-looking lady with a truly handsome nose.

My fingers positively itched to put her nose in my Idea Book, though I don't usually draw real people. It's too hard to get a likeness. I can do pretty good on bits of people, like noses, but when I put them all together, it doesn't always look right.

"It is warm, isn't it?" said Mrs. Benton, taking off her hat and fanning herself.

The door opened from the vestibule at the end of the car and a silver-haired gentleman came through, the one I met on the way to the washroom.

I slunk down in my seat and hoped he wouldn't notice me, which he didn't.

He marched down the aisle, but before he sat down

beside a tall young lady, he looked back at Mrs. Benton and Buster, still hooked up to his harness. Buster smiled at him, a perfectly angelic smile.

"Never figured there was any call to leash up a boy like a dog," he said in a loud voice.

"Buster is a very active child, sir!" Mrs. Benton said.

"Colonel, madam. Colonel Spencer, at your service." The Colonel's voice was about as loud as Pastor Needham's back home. Nobody with tender eardrums ought to sit next to Pastor. Or Colonel Spencer either.

"It's good for a boy to show spirit," the Colonel boomed on. "As my friend General Arthur Gerard used to say, 'A man or a horse without spirit ain't worth a bucket of spit'."

"Indeed," said Mrs. Benton in a chilly voice that could have come straight down from the North Pole.

"Forgive me, madam. The general was a trifle blunt of speech. May I introduce my daughter, Miss Eleanor Spencer."

Miss Eleanor was the tall young lady. She looked as though she wanted to shrink into the red plush seat, but she turned and nodded. Miss Eleanor was pretty (though not as pretty as Damaris).

The Colonel patted Buster on the head. "A fine lad you've got there, Mother."

"Mrs. Benton," she said. Buster blew a spit bubble and knocked Mrs. Benton's pocketbook off the seat.

"Allow me, madam," the Colonel said, bending

over to pick it up. The Colonel wore a ruffled shirt, a fancy embroidered vest, and a gun belt complete with a pearl-handled pistol.

"Custom-made," Joel whispered, eyeing the Colonel's pistol, not his stomach, which was rather substantial.

As we racketed along, I stared out the window at the wheat fields and the sky and wondered if Papa wore a custom-made gun like the Colonel's.

Buster pounded on the window and said, "Bang!"

Mrs. Benton said, "Careful, darling, we mustn't break the glass."

Then to me she said, "I'm sure you're going to be a big help with the children, Abby."

Philippa stared at me. She's really skinny, with little-bird bones. But I oughtn't make any remarks about *anybody* being thin, since I'm on the toothpick side myself. Philippa wore spectacles that were too big and slid down her nose. I smiled at both girls. Rose smiled back. Philippa didn't.

"We must all keep our eyes on Buster." Mrs. Benton smoothed back his curls. "He's such an active child. His father says it's the sign of a superior intelligence."

The superiorly intelligent Buster didn't need any of our eyes on him for long. He climbed up on an empty seat across from the Colonel and fell asleep with his thumb in his mouth.

"The sleep of innocence," said the Colonel.

"Buster sat on Mama's hat," Rose said.

"Did he indeed?" The Colonel chuckled. "I've seen a few ladies' hats could do with that young gentleman's services."

"He bites," said Philippa.

"He used to bite, dear," said Mrs. Benton. "He hasn't done that for ever so long."

"That's because I bit him back," said Philippa.

"Poor dear," said Mrs. Benton. I didn't know if she was talking about Philippa or Buster.

The train rocked and swayed, wheels clacking on the rails. Outside, there was nothing to see but wheat fields, blue sky, and the telegraph poles and rails stretching west. The Colonel had gone to sleep. I could hear him snore.

Mrs. Benton opened a satchel and distributed cookies and books to Philippa and Rose and then traded seats with me so she could talk with Damaris.

Philippa didn't read. Instead she stared at me over her spectacles.

"What's your name?" she asked.

"Abby."

"I know that. What's your whole name?"

"Abigail Keturah Edwards. What's yours?"

"Philippa Ann Benton. I was named for my grandmother on my father's side, who was scalped by Indians. Who were you named for?"

"For two ladies in the Bible," I said. Actually I never much cared for my name, though it would have been worse if Papa had had his way.

He wanted to call me Independence Day Edwards because I was born on the Fourth of July. Mama held out for Abigail Keturah, which I don't much like, but it is certainly a little less positively mortifying than Independence Day Edwards!

"Mama says you're going to live with your father and stepmother," Philippa said.

"That's right."

"Do you like your stepmother?"

"I don't know. I haven't met her yet."

"My birthday is April fifteenth," she said. "I am eight years old. How old are you?"

"Thirteen. Almost thirteen."

I could hear Mrs. Benton saying to Damaris, "I understand your father's been in mining."

"Yes." Damaris looked uneasy. With Papa you're never exactly sure where he is or what he's doing.

"Our papa is a doctor," Philippa announced.

"It must be hard to have him get up at night, people calling sick and all," Damaris said.

"Dr. Benton isn't a medical man," Mrs. Benton said. "He's a professor. Of anthropology."

"He's been to the Fiji Islands studying the aborigines. They used to be cannibals," Philippa said, peering over the glasses sliding down her nose. "They cooked missionaries in pots."

"I declare I don't know where Philippa gets some of her ideas," Mrs. Benton said. "Push your spectacles up, dear. I tell her to eat carrots, to improve her vision, you know, but she has a mind of her own."

Well, Philippa and I agreed on one point anyway. I couldn't stand carrots either at her age, and they still aren't my favorite food.

"I'm afraid weak eyes run in Dr. Benton's side of the family. He wears spectacles too."

"Spectacles?" Colonel Spencer opened his eyes, "On a child? Pity," he said, peering at Philippa, who glared back at him. "But how fortunate, Mother . . ."

"Mrs. Benton."

"How fortunate, madam, that our paths have crossed. I have the honor of representing Dr. Elihu Horton, a fine physician of the homeopathic persuasion. I have in my sample case his excellent specific for ophthalmia or weak eyes."

"The Colonel is a drummer," Joel whispered to me with a grin as the Colonel droned on.

"A drummer?"

"A traveling salesman."

There was a sudden thump and crash.

Buster had awakened and discovered the Bentons' lunch.

THREE

Buster hopped up and down on the seat, happily watch-
ing apples and hard-boiled eggs bobble down the aisle
and milk leak out of a mason jar.

The Colonel leaned back and laughed until tears
came to his eyes while Rose and I chased under seats
and around feet to rescue the rolling fruit.

"Lively little fellow. Mustn't break his spirit,
Mother!" The Colonel's coat flipped open as he felt
around in his back pocket for a handkerchief to wipe
his streaming eyes.

Buster eyed the apples and eggs and the Colonel's
fancy gun belt with equal interest.

"Gun," he said cheerfully.

"Right you are, young fellow." The Colonel wiped
his streaming eyes. "Custom-made with a hair trigger."

"Really, Colonel!" Mrs. Benton eyed the gun with
disapproval.

"It's not loaded, never fear. But about the ophthalmia drops, I assure you these remedies are of the great-

est purity, made according to the most exacting standards, Mother. . . ."

"I'm sorry, no," said Mrs. Benton, mopping milk off Buster, who was flailing away at the window again. "I would have to consult the Professor before applying any medicine to Philippa's eyes."

I decided to put the Colonel and Buster in my Idea Book. I didn't know about Miss Eleanor. She was pretty, but there was nothing else to notice about her. It was as though she were part of the Colonel, attached to him like his embroidered vest or his gun belt, only they were more *rememberable*. That is not a word. I made it up.

Joel kept disappearing, but he reappeared instantly when Damaris opened our lunch basket. I told him he must have "food-sniffer antennae."

He said. "Likewise, sprout!"

Aunt Eunice had packed us crispy fried chicken, pickles, and her special potato salad, the kind she makes with bacon grease, vinegar, mustard, and onions. There was a lot of stuff that would keep longer too: canned sardines and hard-boiled eggs and such.

Our train didn't have a dining car. It stopped every hundred miles or so to take on water and coal or to let passengers off to eat at station cafés. Sometimes in towns people came out and banged on triangles and held up signs advertising BACON AND EGGS or GOOD EATS.

Damaris offered the Bentons some of our food, since

milk had sopped into most of their sandwiches, but Mrs. Benton said they had enough left for lunch and after that they would get off to eat at the station cafés.

The Colonel complained about all our stops, espe-cially the flag stops right out in the middle of nowhere to take on passengers or freight. He kept looking at his watch and saying we were taking forever, though it would only take us four days to get to San Francisco. Before the railroad was built, it took three months by ox team to cross the plains if folks were lucky. Longer if they weren't.

After the lunch stop, Mrs. Benton put Buster down on the empty seat in front of me for a nap. He didn't go to sleep. Instead he climbed up and dangled by his middle on the seat back and blew spit bubbles at me while I wrote in my Idea Book. While I *tried* to write in my Idea Book. When he finished blowing bubbles, he started wiggling his ears.

"However does he do that?" I asked Philippa.

"Papa taught him," she said. "Papa tries to teach Buster lots of things. Papa says he can hardly wait to teach him how to climb mountains and fish and shoot guns."

"No!" I said.

"Yes," she said.

What a totally alarming idea!

As the afternoon wore on, it got hotter and hotter.

I wished I could get out and stand under the pipe when we took on water, but instead Damaris and I wet down our handkerchiefs at the watercooler and put them on our wrists and foreheads to try and keep cool. Miss Eleanor dampened hers with toilet water. Joel and the Colonel didn't dampen theirs with anything.

We all looked about fried and as limp as dishrags, except for Damaris. She was wearing a heavy old brown serge traveling dress the same as I was, so she must have been as hot.

"Your sister is so young and pretty," Miss Eleanor said, obviously noting how cool Damaris looked. "And she acts very responsible."

I nodded. Since Mama died, Damaris has acted *too* responsible, as though it were her job to take care of Joel and me, to make sure that our ears were clean and we didn't have green stuff in our teeth and such.

Mrs. Benton began trying to open her window, but it seemed to be stuck.

"Allow me, madam," said the Colonel.

He got quite red in the face tugging at it until Mrs. Benton told him please not to bother, as she did not want him to have an attack of apoplexy. He didn't give up, though, and when it opened an inch, Mrs. Benton said that was quite good enough. All she wanted was a breath of air.

We all needed air. Our car was only half-full, which was fortunate because most of our fellow passengers must have been on board quite a while. At least they smelled that way. I guess they didn't know there was water in the washroom or didn't know water was good for washing.

Miss Eleanor smelled all right, though, like a flower garden. The Bentons smelled all right too. Except for Buster sometimes.

Eventually Joel disappeared again. The Colonel put a handkerchief over his face and appeared to be taking a nap, and Damaris asked Mrs. Benton if there were many opportunities for stenographers in San Francisco.

"But surely," Mrs. Benton said, "you needn't worry about working, with your father there to take care of you."

"Mama always said we should be able to take care of ourselves," Damaris said.

The Colonel popped out from under his handkerchief and said, "No young woman should go out and soil herself by working in the world of *commerce*."

"Soil herself?" Damaris said sharply. She is very proud of having graduated from Mr. Perkins's Business School at the top of her class.

"A young woman should go from the protection of her father's house to her husband's," said the Colonel.

"Not everyone is fortunate enough to be in that position, Colonel," said Mrs. Benton

"Pity," said the Colonel. Miss Eleanor looked down at her hands and didn't say anything.

Philippa and Rose had pulled out slates and books and paper dolls to keep themselves amused. Philippa was working sums on her slate, and Rose was drawing a birthday cake.

She added balloons to her drawing along with the cake and candles. "I love birthday parties!" she said. "Will you have a birthday party in San Francisco, Abby?"

"I don't know," I said.

"Of course you will, Abby!" Damaris said. "I'm sure Papa will remember your birthday."

I looked down at my hand and twisted my ring; Mama had given it to me last year on my birthday. I blinked hard. Mama never forgot birthdays.

Papa never remembered, except for Damaris's sometimes.

"What's wrong with your eyes?" Philippa asked.

"I got a cinder in them," I said, fishing a handkerchief out of my pocket.

"You're crying," she said.

"I am not," I said, and blew my nose.

"The honk of the wild goose," Joel said, walking back into the car with a grin. I punched him on the arm.

"I'm wounded to the quick," he said, clasping a hand to his heart.

"You are not!"

Then I grinned too. Joel tries to make me laugh when he knows I'm missing Mama, or worrying. He misses Mama too, though he tries not to let on.

"What are we going to call her, Joel?" I asked.

"We'll think of something." He knew who I was talking about: Mrs. MacKay, the lady Papa was going to marry. Or maybe the one he had already married.

"Not Mama!" I said.

"No, not Mama."

I was still feeling totally melancholy when Mrs. Benton screamed.

Buster was trotting down the aisle toward the vestibule door as fast as his chubby legs would carry him.

At the door he stopped and squatted down on his heels.

"The spittoon!" shrieked Mrs. Benton.

I leaped to my feet and raced down the aisle.

As soon as I had seen Buster head for the spittoon, I knew what he was going to do. And he did.

He reached in and pulled out somebody's perfectly disgusting old chaw of tobacco and was examining it with great interest.

Behind me, I heard Philippa say, "He's going to eat it and die!"

Buster grinned up at me.

"No, Buster!" I said.

"Ess!" he said cheerfully.

FOUR

Buster didn't die.

I grabbed his wrist just in time. Two seconds more and that perfectly disgusting chunk of tobacco would have been in his mouth.

He didn't howl, but I surely didn't know what to do with him. His hands were filthy, and he had a smear on his shirtfront and his cheek.

The Colonel laughed until his stomach shook. Then he wiped his eyes and said, "Tobacco has well-known therapeutic values when applied externally."

"But not internally! And certainly not second-hand!" Mrs. Benton said, producing some squares of old sheeting she carries in her satchel for wiping Buster off in emergencies.

"He needs scrubbing," said Rose, wrinkling her nose.

"He needs scouring!" said Philippa.

"You do need a bit of a wash, don't you, my pet?" Mrs. Benton said. "Abby, will you help me?"

"Yes, ma'am," I said. Aunt Eunice would say Mrs. Benton looked "done in." Her hair was coming out from her bun in little wisps.

"Thank you, dear," she said as I helped harness Buster up, and we headed for the washroom.

Buster scooted on ahead, dragging *us* along by the leash. When we passed the little room where the porter shines shoes, he stopped short and scrunched down to look under the half-door, then started tearing down the aisle again. And no sooner had we got to the washroom than he started banging on the lever of the commode and looking down the hole trying to watch the railroad tracks go by.

I held him while Mrs. Benton scrubbed. Buster didn't help. He wriggled and squirmed and wouldn't hold still for two whole minutes running, but between us we finally got him washed off and into a clean sailor suit.

Mrs. Benton stayed in the washroom to scrub *herself* off while Buster and I went back to our car.

Actually we didn't go directly back. I wanted to see the Pullman car, but we got chased out by the porter, who said, "You children go along back where you belong." As though I were the same age as Buster!

At night the porter makes up beds called berths in a Pullman car. We didn't have berths in our chair car. We were going to sleep sitting up (or slumped over on one another). It costs thirteen dollars extra to go by Pullman, so I guess we never will unless we strike it rich.

Mrs. Benton had brought pillows and blankets for the children, but we hadn't thought of it. When night came, we could rent pillows from the porter, but we had decided we'd best not spend the money, though Joel said we'd probably wake up feeling as though we'd been folded up in an accordion.

There was a fifteen-minute stop for water and coal in the late afternoon. Joel and I got off to stretch our legs. We walked two blocks to the end of the wooden sidewalks at the edge of town. The land was still flat as a pancake, with no sign of mountains.

"I thought we could see the Rockies by now," I said.

"They're up ahead, all right, Abby," Joel said. "The land is rising gradually. We're higher than you think."

After the water stop the Colonel started ticking off the towns we passed on the timetable, and he began to tell awful stories about that part of Kansas and about all the men killed while the railroad was being built.

"What happened to them?" Philippa asked.

"Scalped," said the Colonel. "Indians didn't take kindly to our killing off the buffalo."

"Bluffalo," said Buster.

"Buffalo, young man. Buff-a-lo."

"Bulafalo," said Buster, pointing out the window.

"No, dear," said Mrs. Benton. "It's just a horse."

"Indian," said Buster, waving at the rider.

"Fine observant lad you've got there, Mother," said the Colonel, chuckling.

"It's Mrs. Benton, Daddy," Miss Eleanor said in her soft voice, with an apologetic glance at Mrs. Benton.

"Don't fuss, daughter. That's the trouble with you females," said the Colonel. "Always making a pimple out of a molehill." (I think he meant it the other way around.)

Joel winked at me. "How would you like the Colonel for a papa?" he whispered.

"Not much," I said.

We were rather glad when the Colonel went out to smoke. He came back saying he'd met a very interesting retired railroad gentleman named Mr. Peabody.

Joel had met Mr. Peabody too. He said Pea Body was the wrong name for the gentleman. It should have been Mr. Bean Body—Mr. *Lima* Bean Body—because that's the way he was shaped.

When the Colonel came back from talking to Mr. Peabody, he had even *awfuller* stories about train smashes.

"Please, Daddy, don't . . ." Miss Eleanor said nervously.

"Don't be squeamish, daughter," he said, and went right on about boiler explosions and trestles collapsing.

I began to think maybe Miss Eleanor seemed sort of unfinished because of the way the Colonel treated her, not even letting her finish her sentences.

I watched the telegraph poles rush past . . . only it's the other way around. *We* were rushing past the poles. I was thinking about different things. About Papa. And Mrs. MacKay. Wondering if they were married yet and what we should call her if they were.

Then I started thinking about becoming a scientist like Madame Curie in France or an author like Louisa M. Alcott.

Maybe if I did, Papa would be proud of me and love me as much he does Damaris, though I'm not as pretty. Or like me as much as he does Mrs. MacKay.

Rose cuddled up and smiled at me.

"What are you thinking about, Abby?" she asked.

"Papas."

"My papa has a mustache," she said.

"Mine does too."

"It tickles." Rose giggled. "It tickles when he kisses me. Does your papa's mustache tickle you?"

"No," I said. I couldn't remember Papa ever kissing me, but I didn't tell Rose that.

At the supper stop, when Joel and I got out to stretch our legs again, we saw the Colonel talking a mile a minute to the railroad gentleman. (Joel was right. He did look like a Mr. Bean Body.)

Miss Eleanor wasn't with them. I didn't think

much of it until the Colonel came huffing and puffing up to us.

"Have you seen Miss Eleanor?" he asked.

We said we hadn't.

"I think she must have gone to the . . . ah . . ." He hesitated. "The sanitary facility. She'll miss the train if she doesn't hurry."

"I'll get her," I said.

Someday I might learn to mind my own business and not go around being so helpful, but I don't expect anybody should hold their breath until then.

I galloped off to the "sanitary facility" (it was just a little outhouse at the rear of the eating shed) and banged on the door with its little crescent-shaped hole.

"Miss Eleanor!" I called. "Hurry up! The train's leaving!"

The door opened, and a bearded stranger stepped out, adjusting his trousers, and grinned at me.

"The name ain't Eleanor," he said.

"Sorry," I sputtered, turning, I'm sure, all shades of purple with embarrassment.

Then the whistle hooted.

"Sorry," I said again, and, abandoning Miss Eleanor to her fate, I turned to run for the train.

That's when I did it.

I stepped smack-dab in a chuckhole. My ankle folded under me. And there I was, plunked down in the middle of nowhere, my nose stuck in the dirt.

The whistle hooted again.

The conductor on the station platform called out, "Aaaallll a-board!" and then, feeling humorous, he added, "If you can't get aboard, get a plank."

I didn't think it was funny at all!

I thought it was Purely Awful!

FIVE

The bearded stranger helped me scramble up, torn stockings, skinned knees (which was *utterly humiliating!*), and all.

"There you be, girlie!" he said. "Bust anything?"

"I don't think so . . . thanks," I said, testing my ankle.

The whistle hooted again.

"Come on, Abby!" Joel yelled. "Run!"

I was running! As fast as I could go. And bawling. The cars were moving, and all I could think was, What if I miss the train? What if I get stuck right out here in the middle of *nowhere*?

I was gasping for breath when Joel and the conductor reached down and pulled me aboard, and there was an acid, burning taste in my mouth as though my stomach had half a mind to come up to say hello to my tongue.

"Listen for the whistle next time, miss," the conductor said. "You shouldn't wander off in a daydream." I was too out-of-breath to tell him I hadn't been.

"Caught yourselves a big fish that time, boys!" the Colonel said, laughing heartily.

I glared at him. It was his fault, his and Miss Eleanor's, that I almost missed the train.

Damaris gave me one of her Elder Sister lectures, and Mrs. Benton said I'd about given her heart failure, as she felt responsible for delivering me safely into Papa's hands.

The Colonel laughed some more and said I had been "quite a sight."

And Miss Eleanor hadn't been lost at all! She was right there in her seat. She blushed and didn't say one word about where she'd been.

But the Colonel did. He told everybody. She'd gotten herself locked in the washroom when we came into town, and that's where she spent the whole time. I don't know what was worse for her. Getting locked in, or the Colonel talking about it. He seemed to think it was Very Funny.

Miss Eleanor leaned back and shut her eyes as though she were asleep, though I think she was just pretending.

"Papas sometimes do embarrassing things, don't they?" Rose whispered. "Our papa likes old bones. He keeps them in the dining room cupboard, so there's no room for Mama's good dishes. Does your papa do anything peculiar, Abby?"

I felt like saying my Papa *was* peculiar because he hardly ever came home, but I didn't. I just said I didn't know him well enough to say.

We found out more about Miss Eleanor that evening. Actually Philippa did. If I asked as many questions as she did, Aunt Eunice would have had my scalp. Miss Eleanor didn't seem to mind.

Not that there's an awful lot to know about Miss Eleanor, but she told us all about it anyway. She even told us she and the Colonel imported their underwear (she called them undergarments) from Paris, France. If Miss Eleanor thought we'd be interested in her or the Colonel's fancy imported silk underwear, she doesn't have anything too much to talk about, does she?

I didn't tell her that Mama used to order our chemises and bloomers from Sears, Roebuck until she decided it was more economical to make them out of bleached flour sacks.

Katie Malone's ma made her bloomers out of sugar sacks, but she didn't bleach them. When Katie turned a somersault, you could see PURE SUGAR printed on the seat of you-know-where. I would have been so *mortified!* Katie pretended she didn't mind, but I think she did, because she quit turning somersaults.

Miss Eleanor had never kept house, or worked at all. She went to a finishing school, but all she learned there was how to speak French and embroider pillowcases.

"Is that all?" I asked.

I didn't think it was such a Purely Awful thing to say, but maybe it was, because Damaris gave me that Look that means "Shut up."

Miss Eleanor started to say something else, but the Colonel didn't let her finish.

"They taught you to be a gracious ornament to society, daughter. That's all that's necessary for you to know."

Miss Eleanor said, "Yes, Daddy," but she didn't look altogether happy. She didn't seem to want to talk anymore, so I took out my writing case.

"What are you going to do?" Philippa asked.

"Write a letter home," I said.

"It must be awful hard work," she said, peering at me over her glasses.

"It's not easy."

It was trying to be careful about what I said that made writing Dolly hard. Whatever I tell her she's certain positive to tell Mary Margaret Vincent. Dolly does like to talk.

Joel says, "There might as well be a funnel between Dolly Raymond's ears and her mouth!"

That's an awful thing for him to say. Before we left Estes, Dolly was starting to act really silly when Joel was around. Mary Margaret did too. In fact, when *any* boy was around, they both acted tremendously silly. I told them they talked like their brains had turned to soup.

Mary Margaret said, "Boys don't care for girls with brains."

"You mean," I said, "you have to go around all your life pretending you don't have any?"

It does seem practically impossible to pretend forever to be something you're not.

I wondered if Papa liked ladies with brains. Mama was smart. Mrs. MacKay had a business, so she must be too. Would Papa like me better if I pretended I didn't have any? So far, he didn't know me well enough to know if I had a brain or not.

"Your forehead looks like a washboard," Philippa said, her eyes fixed on me like glue. "Mama says ladies will get to looking like prunes if they wrinkle up their foreheads like you do."

I gave a sigh, quit trying to write my letter, and instead started thinking about a new Amaryllis story. One with Buster in it. He could be a fat baby gnome who falls into a hole in the ground and finds a treasure of gold. I did a little drawing for the story in my Idea Book.

Miss Eleanor looked over my shoulder and said, "Why, it's Buster, isn't it? You've caught the likeness, Abby."

We stopped again for water, not at a town, but at a water tower sitting all by itself by the tracks, and the Colonel started complaining again. He told the conductor he must be routing us to Denver by way of Timbuktu, which isn't possible, of course, Timbuktu being in Africa, not Kansas.

Miss Eleanor looked embarrassed but didn't say anything. Joel said it wouldn't do a bit of good if she did. You might as well try to plug the leak in the bottom of the ocean as to try and shut the Colonel up.

The conductor is the boss of the train and wears a handsome uniform and has gold braid on his cap. He said we should be in Denver in the morning.

"High time!" said the Colonel.

Buster was busy playing with a little wooden train set and chewing on his harness.

Rose looked up from her paper dolls and said, "Do sandwiches grow on trees in the Sandwich Islands, Abby?"

I said I thought it was unlikely.

Philippa said of course they didn't. That Captain Cook who discovered them named them in honor of some British gentleman called the Earl of Sandwich, and that now they're called the Hawaiian Islands.

"They have lots of beaches in the Sandwich Islands— I mean the Hawaiian Islands. We're going there after we get home. Papa is going to take us," Rose said.

"They have volcanoes. The people eat fish and coconuts and roast pigs. Probably Buster will fall in one of the volcanoes and get roasted." Philippa didn't look very worried about Buster's fate.

"Maybe we'll take you with us to watch Buster. So he won't get roasted," said softhearted Rose.

"It's not likely," I said.

"We're going there because our papa wants to study the Polynesian culture, and he likes to take us with him," Philippa said. "He misses us when we're gone."

Philippa didn't mean anything by that remark, I told myself. She didn't know Papa wasn't real . . . fatherly. I was just sensitive about him. I stared out the window at the rails taking us closer to Papa.

The Colonel was taking another nap. I could hear him snore.

"Play quietly, Buster dear," Mrs. Benton said. Then she leaned back and shut her eyes, though how she could sleep I don't know, because Buster had begun to run his little wooden cars up and down the back of the seat, saying, "Choo-choo. Choo-choo train."

After crashing the cars together he started chewing on his harness. Then he pressed his nose up against the window, making a smeary print on the glass.

"Indian!" said Buster, tugging at the window.

All of a sudden the window shot up, and there was Buster dangling his harness in the wind.

"Buster!" shrieked Mrs. Benton.

"Bulafalo!" he crowed cheerfully as he leaned out and slung the harness in the general direction of a cow.

I leaped up and caught him by his shirttail and the seat of his pants. Otherwise the Pride of the Bentons would surely have fallen out onto his head and come to an unfortunate end.

The Colonel was awake now and laughed until tears came to his eyes. "Boys will be boys," he said, reaching into his back pocket for a handkerchief so his coat flipped open to show his embroidered waist-coat, his plump round middle, and his gun belt.

"Gun," said Buster, wriggling down from the seat.

"Right you are." The Colonel pulled his fancy custom-made pistol with the hair trigger out of the holster. "Got my name carved right there on the barrel. You want to see it, sonny?"

"Oh, Daddy, please don't . . ." Miss Eleanor said as she pleated her lace-trimmed handkerchief nervously.

"I really don't think that's wise, Colonel," said Mrs. Benton.

"Not to worry, Mother," said the Colonel. "It's not loaded."

"Gun," said Buster with interest.

"Pistol," said the Colonel, handing it over.

"But, Daddy . . ." Miss Eleanor dropped her balled-up hankie to the floor.

"Don't fuss, daughter," the Colonel said as he bent over to pick up Miss Eleanor's handkerchief.

"Bang," said Buster with a gleam in his eye.

And then he pulled the trigger.

SIX

"I'm killed!" bellowed the Colonel, but he wasn't.

Everyone said it could have been worse. Everyone except the Colonel, whose striped silk imported French underwear won't ever be the same again. Neither will the seat of his pants.

That was where Buster shot him.

After that the Colonel didn't call Buster a "lively little fellow." He called him an "imp from Hades" and used words Aunt Eunice washed mouths out with laundry soap for saying.

The Colonel was hollering for a doctor while Miss Eleanor and Mrs. Benton screamed and shrieked and wrung their hands.

Nobody was doing anything about Buster and that gun, so I said (without thinking), "Give Abby the gun, Buster!"

(If I'd thought, I wouldn't have said it.)

Buster smiled happily and said, "No!"

I fixed my hypnotic eye on him (I haven't been a

mother's help for nothing) and said, "Give it to me, Buster."

Buster grinned again and pointed the gun straight at my chest.

"Bang!" said Buster.

The gun clicked but didn't fire.

It took me a minute to figure out that all my bits and pieces were together and I was still alive.

"The gun, Buster," I said weakly.

"Please, Babby?"

"Please, Buster," I said, and he handed it over with a cheerful smile. I took it *very* gingerly, but Buster had used up the last shot on the Colonel.

The conductor had come in and was trying to calm everybody down, especially Miss Eleanor and the Colonel.

"Colonel," the conductor said, "you are a fortunate man. There is a doctor aboard."

"Send him along! What are you standing there jaw-ing for, man? I'm dying," the Colonel said, though he wasn't, of course.

"I'll send *her* right along," the conductor said.

"Her!?" the Colonel bellowed.

"Dr. Merrick is a very fine physician," said the conductor.

"I won't have any female sawbones laying a hand on me," said the Colonel.

"Now, Daddy," said Miss Eleanor, "be sensible."

"Your wound should be attended to before we reach Denver, Colonel, or no telling but what mortification will set in," said the conductor, never cracking a smile.

I think mortification had already set in for the Colonel. The lady doctor came, and the conductor held up a blanket so the rest of us couldn't see while she removed the bullet from the Colonel's you-know-where.

All the while the Colonel kept muttering about "hen doctors" and saying, "It's humiliating, that's what it is. Downright humiliating."

The Colonel certainly made an awful fuss. Ladies have to go to gentlemen doctors all the time, and they don't go around calling them "male sawbones" or "rooster doctors."

After Dr. Merrick left, the Colonel groaned and said he'd have "a proper doctor check the injury out" when he got to Denver.

"We must send Mr. Jerome a telegram telling him we'll be delayed, Daddy!" Miss Eleanor said.

"We'll do nothing of the sort!"

"But, Daddy," she said, "we're expected."

"Well," said the Colonel testily, "you'll just have to go on by yourself!"

"But I must stay with you."

"I forbid it!" The Colonel reared up as much as he was able to and then said, "I'm sure Mrs. Benton will see you safely to the city, Eleanor."

"Of course," murmured Mrs. Benton.

The Colonel groaned as the train creaked and rattled and said, "My dear lady, that takes a load off my mind."

Joel grinned and whispered, "The Colonel needs a load taken off more than his mind!"

"But, Daddy," said Miss Eleanor, "it will be so awkward."

"You'll have to manage, Eleanor," the Colonel said, and he sounded annoyed.

I guess it's all right for young ladies to be "purely ornamental" until something happens, and then they have to be useful. It makes it very confusing. I wondered if Papa thought Damaris and I should be ornamental or useful. Or both.

"I expect you to do your duty, Eleanor," the Colonel said.

"I'll see to her, Colonel," said Mrs. Benton. "Rest easy on that score." (I think it must have been difficult for him to rest at all!)

"Lord have mercy," the Colonel groaned as the train bumped and clacked along the track.

He complained so much that Miss Eleanor arranged for him to take a berth in the Pullman car for the night so he could stretch out on his stomach, though I guess he wasn't very comfortable even so.

The next morning we crossed over into Colorado and caught our first glimpse of the Rockies, pale and far off like a dream. By the time we got to Denver they stood out to the west, sharp and snowcapped against the sky.

Joel said Denver is a thousand miles west of Chicago, almost fifteen hundred miles east of San Francisco, located on a level plain 5,250 feet above sea level.

Joel is a perfect *fountain* of information that I don't always care to hear.

We changed trains at Denver. The last we saw of the Colonel he was being trundled off to an ambulance to see a "regular doctor." Miss Eleanor watched him go. She was still tearing up her handkerchiefs and likely not to have a hankie to her name by the time we reached San Francisco.

The Denver station was a big bustling place. Mrs. Benton was afraid to let us out of her sight for fear we'd miss our connection to Cheyenne.

Buster wanted to see the trains get washed. A man stood on the roof of the car with a hose, letting the water stream down over the sides, while men on the ground scrubbed off soot and grime with long-handled brushes.

He watched with interest as the water swished down over the windows. Too much interest, I thought.

"We ought to try to find Buster a new harness," I said, holding on to his shirttail so he wouldn't take a notion to dodge out under the streams of dirty water.

"I doubt if we can find one here," Mrs. Benton said anxiously. "But perhaps a big boy like Buster doesn't need one anymore. Can you be very, very good, dear?"

"Ess!" said Buster, watching the water stream down over the cars.

And he was. For a while.

SEVEN

It was remarkable how angelic Buster could look. When he was asleep!

He took a long nap as the train chugged north toward Cheyenne, which was a mercy, because Mrs. Benton hadn't found a new harness.

"Poor little lamb. A long trip is hard on a child with an active mind like Buster's," she said, smoothing back his curls.

There certainly is a lot of high lonesome land in the West. When I was little, I used to think the states had lines marking off their boundaries, but of course they don't. And the mountains don't have labels stuck on them either.

The retired railroad man, Mr. Peabody, told us that ladies vote in Wyoming just like men. They don't other places. I don't know why not. It doesn't seem fair. Most ladies are as smart as most men. Some are smarter.

Miss Eleanor said, "Daddy says the fair sex—that's

what he calls ladies—shouldn't have to bother their heads over politics."

I said, "Maybe gentlemen are afraid ladies will take their brooms and scrub brushes to the government!"

"Get a soapbox and join the suffragettes, Abby!" Joel said as he peeled the shell off a hard-boiled egg.

"Maybe I just will!" I said.

Suffragettes are the ladies who march around with placards, and chain themselves to fences, and go on hunger strikes demanding the vote. I don't actually know any personally.

I took out my Idea Book and started doing a sketch of the long line of mountains off to the west. I had to work fast because the train kept rolling right along, not waiting for me to get a drawing just right before the view changed.

I wasn't satisfied with the sketch. I knew it wasn't anywhere near as good as what Mrs. Smith Kenyon could do, but Miss Eleanor looked at it and said, "How nice. You are very talented, Abby."

It does make you feel good inside, as though you'd swallowed great dollops of sweet cream, when someone says something nice to you, especially if it's not a relative or someone you know really well who is just being nice.

I am resolved when I am grown to say nice things to young people *if they deserve it*. That's what Uncle George does.

Joel says compliments, the ones you deserve, are "fertilizer for the soul," only he didn't say it quite like that, and Damaris told him "manure for the soul" sounded terribly inelegant.

In Wyoming a band of Indians (*peaceful* Indians) on ponies raced the train. They whooped and hollered, the ponies' manes and tails sailing straight out in the wind.

Buster woke up and kept his nose glued to the window for miles and miles, watching until the Indians finally waved and fell back.

Cheyenne was the dinner stop, and we changed trains again. Two locomotives were hitched together for the climb up to the Continental Divide. That's where when the snows melt on the mountains, some of the water rushes down to the west, to the Pacific Ocean. Some runs east, back toward the Mississippi . . . back toward home . . . toward Estes. I guess it's not home anymore. . . .

"Damaris, Papa will meet us, won't he?" I said.

"Of course," she said.

"But what will we do if he doesn't?"

"He will," said Damaris. I hoped she was right.

When we left Estes, I had told myself everything was bound to be just fine, but the farther west we got, the more I seemed to worry. About Papa. About Mrs. MacKay. What were we going to call her? We couldn't keep calling her Mrs. MacKay.

I kept twisting my ring, the one Mama gave me for

my birthday. Papa forgot my last birthday. He forgot Joel's too. Damaris said that was different. He might forget our birthdays, but he wouldn't forget *us*, but she always thought Papa was Positively Perfect, no matter what.

I wasn't the only one worrying.

Miss Eleanor was too. She didn't say what she was worrying about. She just stared out the window and sighed a lot. And she spent a lot of time in the wash-room. Joel said she was wearing a path through the floorboards going back and forth.

I spent a lot of time there too, but I tended business and left. Miss Eleanor kept looking in the mirror, pinching her cheeks and biting her lips.

She was probably just nervous, but that's what ladies do to make their cheeks and lips red instead of using rouge. I believe if I wanted my lips to look redder, which I don't, but if I did, I wouldn't bite them raw. I'd use lip rouge, though Aunt Eunice says it is wicked and only actresses do.

Dolly and Mary Margaret Vincent sent away for some once, and when they tried it on, their fathers scrubbed their mouths off with laundry soap.

I wondered if Miss Eleanor was worrying about money, because she didn't eat at the station restaurant at Cheyenne but bought a sandwich off the "butch" when he came through.

We crossed the Divide during the night. When we stopped the next morning for coal and water, it was cold. Mrs. Benton bundled the children into coats and hats before letting them out for a run on the platform.

Philippa and Rose went racing off, with Buster trotting along between them. They came back two minutes later without him.

"Brother's lost," wailed Rose.

"Lost?" said Mrs. Benton.

"We found his coat," said Philippa, holding out the woolly garment.

Mrs. Benton was Purely Frantic.

She ordered Rose and Philippa to sit on a bench and not move an inch while she ran around in an absolute tizzy looking for him. Joel and I hunted in the station and among the luggage carts and wagons. It was no use. Buster was gone.

Rose wept and said, "Poor brother! If we can't find him, will the doctor bring us another?"

Philippa said, "Don't be silly, Rose."

I didn't think Damaris, or Mrs. Benton either, would want me to tell Philippa and Rose what I'd found out from reading Aunt Eunice's copy of *What Every Young Woman Should Know*, but I didn't have to.

Philippa looked at Rose over her spectacles and said, "Doctors don't bring babies. Neither does the stork."

"How do they get here?" asked Rose.

"The same way baby chickens do, only they come without shells!"

That left me most entirely speechless.

Before I could think of a single thing to say, the conductor shouted, "All aboard!" and Mrs. Benton still hadn't caught up with Buster.

Damaris said we had to go or we'd miss Papa.

As the train pulled out, we saw Mrs. Benton.

She'd found Buster, all right. He looked a little grimy but angelic as ever with his big blue eyes and blond curls. He waved to Mrs. Benton and the girls, and then to us from the top of the water tower, and it was plain to see there was no chance of their catching the train.

EIGHT

After we left Buster waving at us from that water tower in Wyoming, Damaris fixed her eye on me and said, "*Never* tell Aunt Eunice and Uncle George we had to go on alone!"

"Never?" I said. "Not even after we get there safely?" (which I expected we would).

"Never!" said Damaris.

"No sense worrying them," said Joel, searching through our basket for some crackers and cheese. We had eaten up all the chicken and potato salad.

We weren't actually alone. There were other passengers in the car, but no one we knew except for Miss Eleanor, and she might as well have been on the moon for all the attention she paid us. Dr. Merrick was in the next car. So was Mr. Peabody, the retired railroad gentleman Joel liked to talk to.

As we got closer to Salt Lake, it started to get hot again. Mr. Peabody began telling his train-wreck and boiler-explosion stories to Joel, who said they were "very educational." Horrid is what they were.

Miss Eleanor watched Damaris slide the vestibule door open to go talk to Dr. Merrick. Damaris was spending so much time with her, Joel said maybe she was planning to give up typewriting and take up doctoring.

"Your sister is so capable, Abby," Miss Eleanor said with a sigh.

"Don't you know how to do *anything*, Miss Eleanor?"

I am in *absolute despair*! I just open my mouth and these Purely Awful things come out!

I could have bitten my tongue right off! But it was too late. The words just slipped out like half-cooked jelly off a spoon! Miss Eleanor didn't seem to have noticed.

"There *is* something. Daddy doesn't know," she said. "You mustn't tell him, Abby."

"I won't," I said.

"Promise?"

"Cross my heart." It did seem a little unnecessary with the Colonel back in Denver nursing his wound, but I crossed it anyway. I thought maybe Miss Eleanor was going to tell me why the Colonel made her go on without him, but she didn't.

"It's about my friend Mr. Francis," she said.

"Yes?" I said, smelling Romance with a capital R.

"Chef Francis." She pulled his picture out of her purse. I knew it couldn't be Romance the minute I saw it. Chef Francis is fat with triple chins and a mustache with waxed tips.

"He taught me to cook," said Miss Eleanor as though cooking were a Pure Miracle instead of something most ladies do every day of the week. Excepting Sundays, of course.

"Is that . . . ?"

I was going to say, "Is that all?" but I swallowed the "all" when I saw her face. She looked as if Chef Francis had given her first prize in a chocolate cream-eating contest.

"He taught me how to make bread," said Miss Eleanor. "It was when Daddy had business in New Orleans, before he lost his money and started selling medicines. We lived at a hotel, and Daddy was terribly busy. Chef Francis was very kind. He let me help in the kitchen, and I learned how to cook, mostly breads and desserts. But you mustn't ever tell Daddy that I helped in a kitchen, Abby. He would have a . . ."

"A fit?"

She nodded.

"My lips are sealed," I said.

It really is a puzzle. Some papas are just like roosters, who let the hens lay the eggs and hatch the chicks and don't take a speck of care of the babies themselves.

And then there are papas like Colonel Spencer. He acts as though Miss Eleanor (even if she is a very tall lady) can't swallow mush without he holds open her mouth and stuffs it in.

Our papa, I thought, is more like the rooster.

Then, of course, I had to feel guilty for thinking that! It is terrible to think things and then think you oughtn't to have thought them. I wonder if God is keeping track. It must keep Him most awfully busy!

Miss Eleanor showed me a picture of the Colonel and her mother too. They looked as stiff as though their teeth hurt or they had swallowed pokers. The pictures were mounted on cardboard the size of picture postcards.

I was going to hunt up our picture of Mama and Papa to show her, but Damaris already had.

"Your daddy is quite a handsome man!" she said. "And what an exciting life he's led, going all over this country. I haven't done anything very interesting at all."

Then she asked, "How old is your daddy, Abby?"

"Old," I said. "Forty."

"That's not so old," said Miss Eleanor. "The Colonel is sixty-five. That's why he worries so about my future."

I didn't know why the Colonel should worry so much about Miss Eleanor. She looked healthy to me, and she was taller than the conductor who came through to punch our tickets.

Miss Eleanor had another picture, one of a man with light eyes and a mustache.

"Who is it, Miss Eleanor?"

She looked at the picture, not answering for a minute, as the wheels clicked over the track.

Then she sighed and said, "It's Mr. Quentin Jerome, the man I'm to marry in San Francisco."

Dolly Raymond and Mary Margaret Vincent giggle and flap their eyelashes when they talk about boys they like. And Mrs. Smith Kenyon, who is old and married, acts sort of sweet and giggly with Mr. Smith Kenyon, even when he brings home Brussels sprouts and liver.

Miss Eleanor didn't giggle or flap her eyelashes. She acted more like someone was going to make her eat liver and Brussels sprouts.

She did take down her hatbox, though, and showed me her wedding hat. It was made of lacy straw with silk flowers and ribbons.

"It's very pretty," I said.

"It is, isn't it?" she said, putting it back in the box and cramming the cover on.

"I'd have thought the Colonel would want you to wait until his wound was healed and he could come to your wedding."

"Daddy doesn't want any delay," she said. "He's most anxious. He and Mr. Jerome are to go into business together, but . . ."

She hesitated so long, I said, "But what?"

"It doesn't seem proper for me to stay at Mr. Jerome's without the Colonel, not before we're married. I must find lodging elsewhere."

So, I thought, that was why Miss Eleanor was buying sandwiches off the butch instead of eating at the station restaurants. She was saving money for room rent.

The door to the vestibule slid open. Damaris came through, and Miss Eleanor had to show her the pictures and the hat.

"Is Mr. Jerome meeting you in San Francisco?" Damaris asked.

"Yes. I believe so. I do hope that Mr. Jerome and I . . . that we aren't disappointed in each other. I wish I wasn't quite so . . ." She laughed nervously.

"So tall?" I said.

There I'd done it again!

I surely didn't want to hurt Miss Eleanor's feelings, so I said real quickly, "You have a really pretty face, Miss Eleanor. And nice hands."

Damaris gave me a long Aunt Eunice type lecture later and said, "You don't have to say every single thing that comes into your head, Abby!"

"I know!" I said with a sigh.

What I said to Miss Eleanor was awful! But it's pretty awful too if people don't like you because of how tall you are, or if your nose isn't the right shape.

Or your feet are too big. Sigh.

Damaris is taller than I am, but I have bigger feet. It is a great trial. I had a dream once sort of like that story about Red Riding Hood, only in my dream the wolf looked at me and said, "What enormous big feet you have, Abigail!"

But why, I wondered, had Miss Eleanor said she hoped she and Mr. Jerome wouldn't be disappointed in each other? Hadn't they met?

I was very proud of myself because I hadn't asked, although I was practically *eaten alive* with curiosity.

NINE

We were clear into Utah before we finally finished up the last hard-boiled egg in Aunt Eunice's basket.

"About time!" Joel said. "One more egg and I'd flap my wings and go cock-a-doodle-doo!"

Damaris and Joel (especially Joel) decided we should eat dinner at the next meal stop.

What a disappointment! The eating place was nothing but a big barn out in the middle of nowhere. It was hot and dusty and the flies swarmed in. We had slabs of warmed-over beef, lumpy potatoes, stringy cabbage, followed by pie with a soggy half-done crust, all washed down with weak coffee, and no milk, not even canned.

From then on we stuck with sandwiches and soda pop we bought off the butch. The sandwiches weren't very good either, but they were filling and it was cheaper than eating at the meal stops.

Miss Eleanor kept saying the butch's sandwiches couldn't compare to the ones her friend Chef Francis produced. His, she said, were "masterpieces" made with baguettes (whatever they are, a kind of roll, I think) stuffed with "liver pâté."

I personally can't imagine anything with *liver* in it being good, but Miss Eleanor looks dreamy-eyed just talking about it. More dreamy-eyed than when she talks about Mr. Quentin Jerome, whom she is going to marry in San Francisco.

"Does Mr. Jerome like liver pâté?" I asked.

She said she didn't know. Then I asked what he did like, and she didn't know that either.

She had never ever met Mr. Quentin Jerome!

Marrying him was the Colonel's idea, which I thought was positively *medieval*!

Damaris said it was none of my business, but I decided if ever I am to get married, which I won't, of course, but if I should, I want to see the man first to find out if he has teeth and smells all right and isn't inclined to throw things. My goodness! You don't even buy a watermelon without thumping it!

Joel said I had kept after Miss Eleanor "like a wood-pecker after a nut," and that's how I found out she was to inherit money from her grandmother, her mother's mother, but not until she turned thirty.

Or until she got married. So that's why she was marrying Mr. Jerome, to get her money; but I couldn't figure out how that would help the Colonel, though I could see how it would help Mr. Jerome.

Joel says in lots of places ladies aren't allowed to manage their own money, not unless their husbands are dead, which doesn't seem fair. (I believe I *will* become a suffragette when I am older and march with placards and let myself be chained to fences to protest, and go on hunger strikes. Well, maybe not hunger strikes.)

Miss Eleanor said the Colonel was going into business with Mr. Jerome after the wedding. I guess that's what the Colonel was to get out of it—a job.

"She could at least marry someone she knows!" I said to Joel when Miss Eleanor had gone to the washroom (again).

"Maybe she doesn't know anybody. Or doesn't know anybody who likes tall ladies," Joel said.

"She could go to work!" I said. "Well, maybe she couldn't, not unless someone wants a cook who can only do desserts and bread. But it doesn't seem right. Miss Eleanor is nice. It seems like she could marry somebody she knows."

"Maybe you should find somebody for her, Abby. You can play Daniel Q. Cupid," Joel said.

Later I asked Miss Eleanor, "Why don't you just wait until you're thirty? Then you would have your money and you wouldn't have to marry anybody."

"You don't understand, Abby. We need money now. We only have what Daddy makes selling medicines. And, I'm afraid, that's not enough."

"But . . ." I started to object.

"I tell myself this is really an adventure!" she said firmly.

"Fine adventure!" I muttered, starting to think about Bluebeard killing all his wives in Transylvania and hiding their corpses in his secret room. I didn't really suppose Mr. Jerome was a Bluebeard . . . or was he?

"Daddy says he won't rest easy until I'm married. He says a young woman should go from the protection of her father to that of her husband. . . . Oh, I am sorry." she said, looking flustered.

"Sorry about what?"

"I shouldn't have said that."

"Why not?"

"I forgot. You and Damaris. You haven't had your father to protect you."

"Well, I guess he would if he had to," I said.

I felt sort of stiff, all prickly and insulted. He wasn't perfect, of course (though Damaris thought he was), but we still did have a papa. He said we could come out to California. He hadn't actually deserted us, for heaven's sake!

I did not like someone feeling sorry for us!

Particularly Miss Eleanor, who was in an awful fix herself, if you ask me!

I didn't talk to her anymore, but looked out at the scenery. It was our third day on the train, and there always seemed to be more mountains and more valleys in front of us.

We went through the desert west of Salt Lake that night. I watched the moon and the clouds and the telegraph poles black in the moonlight, and started thinking (again) about Papa . . . and Mrs. MacKay . . . and how maybe it wouldn't be so bad having a step-mother. . . .

In the middle of the night Damaris poked me awake and said I was giving her a crick in her side from leaning on her. I moved over, and she went back to sleep, but I stayed awake listening to the wheels click over the rail joints.

The moon was shining on the desert . . . on a white skull with black eyeholes, the skull of a cow, or maybe an ox that once pulled an emigrant's covered wagon.

Joel said we were lucky to go through the desert at night instead of in the heat of the day, or we might all wind up "desiccated remnants" of our own selves. Dried like human jerky, mummies, or just another pile of white bones bleaching under the sun.

Poor Miss Eleanor! Joel about scared her to death with his talk. I don't believe he meant to. I thought he quite liked Miss Eleanor, but he did like to get a "rise" out of her.

By morning we had reached Reno, and the Sierra Nevada loomed up ahead out of the flat high desert. It was just a big old wall of rock, and I surely couldn't see a way through it, but there was.

As we started up toward the pass, the train slowed down so much it seemed as though we ought to all get out and push. The wheels seemed to be saying over and over again . . . Papa . . . Papa . . . Mrs.

MacKay . . . I guess because I'd been thinking about them so much.

The mountains east of the pass were covered with lumps of sage and scattered pine and reminded me of Aunt Eunice's raisin cake. Everything was bone-dry, but as soon as we crossed into California it started to rain. Lightning bounced off the mountains and split a pine tree by the roadbed right in two.

"Oh, my!" said Miss Eleanor. "I didn't think it was supposed to rain in California."

"We're lucky it's not snowing," Joel said as the thunder rolled off into the distance.

I don't know how any of those emigrants with their covered wagons and oxen ever made it over the mountains.

Some of them didn't. Joel said the Donner Party got stuck somewhere up near the pass all winter and those that lived ate those who didn't, which was too Utterly Horrid to think about, so I didn't.

There were more tunnels, through solid rock, than I could count and miles of wooden snow sheds so the trains could keep going even in winter.

In one place a narrow shelf had been blasted out of rock for the railbed, and it looked as if one good breeze could send the whole train about half a mile down to the river below. And that would be the end of us. We wouldn't have to worry about Papa or Mrs. MacKay or anything forever and ever.

I scooched myself over to an empty seat on the

opposite side of the train. Might be my extra weight making it tip over! Miss Eleanor scootched over too, and we both breathed a most enormous sigh of relief when the shelf widened out.

Joel grinned and said, "We made it!"

The words were no sooner out of his mouth than we felt a tremendous jolt . . . three jolts . . . and a bang.

The train bounced off the track.

We all went flying, screaming as we slammed into seats and into one another, our satchels and suitcases tumbling around us. Then the cars scrunched and jarred to a stop.

TEN

I'm not exactly sure what happened next.

As we slid around helter-skelter, people screamed, babies cried, and a satchel came slamming down from somewhere and banged me on the head.

Our car was tilted over at a most alarming angle, though it hadn't turned over. Among all the confusion, I heard Mr. Peabody, the retired railroad gentleman, who had been in our car talking to Joel, saying, "Keep calm, folks. . . . Keep calm. . . ."

"Damaris! Joel!" I was screaming at the top of my lungs myself.

"We're all right, Abby," Joel called.

People started climbing over seats and crawling for the door. I remember seeing Miss Eleanor's hatbox burst open and somebody's big boot go through her wedding hat.

The car swayed. I hoped it wouldn't tip over on us as we crawled out from under, or we'd be smashed flat.

"The door's jammed!" someone hollered.

"Keep calm, folks! We'll all get out." Mr. Peabody reached up and smashed windows with his cane. Passengers began to climb out and then reached down to help others still trapped in the car.

Joel pushed Damaris through and then turned to me.

"Come on, Abby," he said.

"Wait! Miss Eleanor! Where is she?"

She was out cold.

"Miss Eleanor! Wake up!" I said, which was dumb, since she wasn't asleep.

"We can't leave her, Joel!" I said, but we couldn't budge her an inch, much less lift her.

"Her smelling salts!" I said, searching her pockets.

The bottle hadn't broken, thank goodness, and a couple of whiffs brought her around. We got her on her feet and pushed her out the window (after we pulled off two of her petticoats so she could squeeze through). Then it was my turn. Joel climbed out on his own.

A big chunk of the mountain loosened by the rain had broken away, boulders, trees, and all, and come crashing down on the track ahead of us, luckily not right smack-dab on top of us.

Most of the cars were tilted at odd angles. The baggage car was wrecked, and the locomotive had overturned. It was still hissing steam and looked like a large overturned beetle.

The track would have to be cleared and the engine

and cars set back on it. Joel said they would probably tap into the telegraph line and wire ahead for a replacement train and a repair crew.

"Oh, my!" said Miss Eleanor. "I suppose this means we won't arrive in San Francisco on time."

"Not a chance," Joel said.

"Oh, my," said Miss Eleanor again. "Our trunks?"

"Smashed," said Joel.

Nobody got killed, which was a plain miracle, but there were plenty of bumps and bruises. One of the passengers broke his ankle when he jumped down from his car, and the train fireman, the man who shovels coal into the firebox, got burned. Dr. Merrick was tending to the injured. Damaris went to see if she could help, and when she was gone, Joel crawled back in our car for our satchels and valises.

I sat on a rock and waited it seemed forever. I guess it was pretty near four hours. A river rushed down the canyon below the tracks, water creaming over the rocks. Snowcapped mountains towered around us, and an eagle circled overhead.

Joel said he'd get a telegram off to Papa from the next town, but, I thought, what if Papa didn't get it? What if he couldn't meet us? Damaris said he'd send someone if he couldn't come himself. Were we just supposed to follow some strange man willy-nilly? Someone we didn't know from—"from Adam's off ox," as Uncle George would say.

Then, of course, I had to think about Aunt Eunice

telling us not to talk to strangers and her talking to Dolly Raymond's ma (when they didn't think we were listening) about "white slavery," which seemed to mean *ladies*' slavery (ladies who hadn't been careful about talking to strangers) and sounded horrid.

I watched the eagle and wished I could soar in the sky as it did. I would fly right down the mountain to San Francisco.

Then, to take my mind off Papa and Mrs. MacKay, I started planning a new story about Amaryllis, the Fairy Child, riding on the back of an eagle with feathers of gold. . . .

"Penny for your thoughts," Joel said, plopping down on the rock next to me. "I'll bet you're worrying about Papa again."

"I wasn't until you mentioned him!" I said. We both were quiet for a minute.

"How will we know him, Joel? We haven't seen him for ever so long."

"We have his picture. Don't stew and fret, Abby."

I wasn't the only one stewing and fretting. Miss Eleanor was too.

She kept saying, "We could have been killed." Then she put her hand to her head and said, "I could have been killed. . . ."

"So could we all," said Joel.

"But," said Miss Eleanor, "I haven't done anything I wanted to yet!"

"There's still time to do what you want, Miss Eleanor," I said, patting her hand.

"Do you think so, Abby?"

"Yes," I said, though, of course, Miss Eleanor is twenty-five, which is pretty old.

A replacement train finally came chugging up the mountain. The repair crew got off, and we got on. We had to pick our way across the slide, lugging the satchels and valises Joel had retrieved for us. Miss Eleanor's wedding hat was not retrievable. It was squashed flat.

The new train wasn't really new, but it did get us to the next town, where Joel sent a telegram to Papa, and then down the mountains to Sacramento where we were to wait for another train. From there it would be another five or six hours to San Francisco.

The waiting room was full of people, mostly men, scurrying here and there or standing around smoking fat cigars. Or chewing tobacco and spitting into—and a lot of times missing—the big brass spittoons. Off to one side was a room with a bar, an enormous mahogany affair about a city block long.

"Where's Miss Eleanor?" I asked. "She wanted us to wait for her."

"One guess," said Joel.

"In the washroom."

Damaris wasn't listening. She was staring at a man going toward the bar. A tall man. His hair streaked brown and blond like Joel's.

"What is it, Damaris?" Joel said.

"Papa!" she whispered.

"It isn't!" I said. "Papa's to meet us in San Francisco, not Sacramento."

"There!" Damaris said. "See him? He's turned away from us, but it's Papa. I'm sure it's Papa!"

All three of us went scrambling forward loaded down with our satchels and valises, quite forgetting Miss Eleanor altogether.

Then the tall man turned around and looked our way.

Damaris was right.

We had found Papa.

ELEVEN

"Papa!" Damaris and I screamed.

"He doesn't see us!" I said.

"I'll get him!" Joel dropped his satchel at our feet and charged off through the crowd. We saw him grab Papa by the arm and start dragging him toward us.

"Well, children!" Papa said. "Lucky you spotted me. Mrs. MacKay sent the message on about the train delay, but I never would have recognized you."

"But . . ." Damaris said, "how is it you are in Sacramento, Papa?"

"Fortuitous circumstances, princess. You might say I've been killing a number of birds with one stone. Officially it's business, to check on a cotton order. But look at you! All grown-up and beautiful!"

He twirled her around right in the middle of the station and then kissed her on the cheek.

Papa looked perfectly splendid himself, freshly barbered, shoes shined, snowy shirt with starched collar and cuffs, a diamond stickpin in his tie, and carrying a fancy malacca cane.

He stuck the tip of his cane under my chin and said, "And who might this young lady be? It can't be Abby."

"Oh, Papa! Of course it's me!" I forgave him the cane because he called me a young lady.

"It is *I*," Papa corrected. Then he added, "Sloppy language is an indication of sloppy thinking, chicken."

Chicken!

I thought that was pretty sloppy *speaking*. It wiped out all the good feeling I had about being called a young lady. Papa didn't notice how I felt. He was too busy admiring Damaris. She really is a grown-up young lady and doesn't say, "It is me," instead of "It is I."

I felt positively grimy next to Papa. It's not easy to keep clean in a cubbyhole of a train washroom. Damaris, of course, looked as fresh and cool as a lemon ice.

"So here you all are," Papa said again.

He didn't offer to kiss me.

I think he had his mind on something besides us, because he kept looking over our shoulders toward the room with the long mahogany bar.

"But, Papa," I said, "if you were here, who was going to meet us in San Francisco?"

"Mrs. MacKay would have seen to you," he said. "A most admirable lady. It was a fortunate day for me when we met."

"How did you . . ."

I was going to ask how they did meet, but guessed Damaris would say it was a personal question and send me that "Shut up" look, so I didn't. Papa explained anyway. Sort of.

He said, "I was able to be of some assistance to Mrs. MacKay when her husband died. She was most appreciative. I myself had but recently lost your mother. From such unfortunate circumstances our mutual affections grew."

For a minute he looked as solemn as Pastor Needham back home. Then he said again, quite cheerfully, that it was lucky we had recognized him, as he would never have known us, especially Damaris.

"Are you three hungry?" he asked, looking over our heads toward the bar.

"Yes," said Joel.

"Joel is always hungry," I said.

"So's Abby," Joel said.

"Well, suppose we have the finest dinner Sacramento has to offer."

"Aren't we going on to San Francisco?" I asked.

"Later, Miss Abigail Independence Day Edwards."

Papa looked toward the bar again and said, "Find a seat, youngsters. I do have to see a man about a horse. . . ."

"A horse?" I said as he walked toward the bar.

"Just an expression, Miss Independence Day Edwards!" said Joel.

"Thanks for telling me, Mr. Joel Ezra Amos Edwards," I said, which was the only way I could think of to get even for "Miss Independence Day," but it didn't work. Joel just laughed, and Damaris told us not to fuss.

As we gathered up our belongings and looked for an empty bench in the waiting room, Miss Eleanor stepped down off the train. She was the last one off.

I thought she'd probably gotten herself locked in the washroom again and didn't want to admit it, but she said she'd been talking to the conductor about her trunk. It had been rescued from the smashed baggage car but would have to be sent on later.

When Papa came back, we introduced him. Miss Eleanor blushed and said she was glad to meet him and that she and the Bentons had become quite fond of us on the trip.

"Really?" Papa smiled at her.

"Indeed," said Miss Eleanor, getting even redder.

"Who are the Bentons?" asked Papa.

When we explained how Mrs. Benton was supposed to keep her eye on us, he said, "Leave it to Eunice to find you a warden."

"She worried about us!" (I was surprised at myself for leaping to Aunt Eunice's defense.) "And so did Uncle George!"

"Admirable people," Papa said, a little twist of a smile on his lips.

"Mr. Edwards," Miss Eleanor said, "I wonder if you could recommend lodging in San Francisco?"

"The Palace Hotel is the finest in town."

"It sounds quite grand, but I was thinking of something more modest."

"I stayed at Mrs. Wheeler's boardinghouse before I took rooms near my employment."

"Is it clean?"

"It's clean, all right," Papa said, "but the food is, to put it kindly, on the plain side."

Miss Eleanor said she thought it would do quite well and said we must come to see her.

Then Papa offered to help her with her valises, but she said she could manage by herself, which didn't seem likely to me, knowing Miss Eleanor; but she is a grown-up lady, so we had to leave her there to "shift for herself," as Aunt Eunice would say.

Papa looked back at her. "Pretty girl," he said. "Doesn't know how to dress, though."

I knew Papa didn't mean Miss Eleanor wears her chemise outside her shirtdress, but that she wasn't stylish.

Damaris looked uncomfortable and smoothed down her skirt. We weren't very stylish ourselves in our brown serge traveling dresses.

"It takes money," Damaris said, "to look smart."

"It takes talent. And taste. But it takes hard cash to finance the real work of the world. It takes, dear children, a grubstake."

"A grubstake?" said Damaris.

"Money advanced to further any enterprise. Those

with the money often have little faith in the enterprise."

While Papa talked about money, I thought about
Mama sewing for Mrs. Smith Kenyon and other ladies
when Papa didn't get around to sending us money.
Aunt Eunice used to say it was because he put all his
cash into holes in the ground. She meant mines that
didn't pay off.

"Well," said Joel, "Miss Eleanor ought to have
plenty of money to buy all kinds of fancy duds once
she gets married."

"Come west to marry money, has she?"

"No." Damaris's eyes were flashing bits of fire, but
Papa didn't notice.

I started to explain how Miss Eleanor would inherit
her money when she married and wouldn't have to
wait until she was thirty years old.

"So, your Miss Eleanor is a young woman with
considerable assets," he said as he began to poke at
our valises and satchels with his cane.

"What's all this?" he asked.

When we admitted it was our luggage, he said, "I
see we have a job cut out for us. We'll have to get
rid of this rubbish, or Molly will think you came from
an orphan home."

"Molly?" I said.

"Mary, but I call her Molly. Mrs. MacKay, your
future stepmother."

"You aren't married yet?"

"No." Papa frowned. "Not yet. In the meantime" —he poked my straw valise—"we'll consign this semi-precious cargo to the check stand. Then we'll eat." He began to lead us toward the entrance through the jostling crowd.

"My, what a press of people," Damaris said, wrinkling her nose at the smell of sweat, cigars, and whiskey. I felt as if I were about to drown in people myself.

"Town is full of hangers-on," said Papa. "This is the state capital."

Sacramento is on the river between two ranges of mountains, but we couldn't see either one. It was hot. I guess it was the heat haze that hid the mountains.

We had lunch at a hotel dining room cooled by fans in the ceiling. The tables were covered with white cloths, and the napkins were folded in fancy shapes and stuck in the water glasses. The lunch was very expensive. I hoped Papa had enough money to pay for it. I guess I was frowning some because he looked at me and quit smiling.

"What is it, Papa?" asked Damaris.

"The oddities of heredity never fail to astound me, princess. Abigail here is my mother's mother, all over again. Yes, she's the spitting image of the old lady."

Well, that really spoiled my lunch. How, I kept wondering, could I look like Papa's old grandmother, who died when she was ninety and didn't have a tooth in her head?

Papa probably didn't remember I was thirteen. Almost thirteen. I wished he would. I watched him cut his chop. His hands surely didn't look like a miner's hands, and I wondered what sort of work Papa did for Mary MacKay.

He saw me looking at his hands and said, "Lost my calluses. Been hitched to a desk too long."

Joel was quiet and didn't say more than two words. He hadn't had much opportunity, because Papa talked a lot. He told us all about the city, about the levees built by Chinese laborers to keep the city from being flooded every year by the water coming down from the Sierra. Chinese laborers helped build the railroad too.

Maybe Joel felt put out of place, and that's why he wasn't saying much. Mama always said he had to be the man of the family while Papa was away. Now he was back to being a kid again.

After we left the hotel dining room, Papa parked us in the lobby and told us to wait for him because he had to attend to some business.

We sat and sat. At least Damaris and I sat and sat. Joel got up and prowled around the lobby. There was a clock over the desk, and the minutes just crawled by. The room clerk kept looking at us. Or at Damaris, more likely.

"We are going to miss the train," I said.

"It doesn't matter. We've found Papa," Damaris said.

"Miss Eleanor will probably make it."

"Probably," said Damaris.

"How much longer do you think this business of Papa's is going to take?"

"I'm sure I don't know," she said.

I looked at her out of the corner of my eye. I couldn't figure out what was ailing her, but it wasn't improving her disposition any. Damaris has always thought Papa was absolutely perfect. I wondered if she was changing her mind.

The clock kept ticking away.

"Uncle George wouldn't have left us like this," I said.

Damaris made an impatient motion with her hand, and Joel said, "He would if he had to, Abby."

"If we do miss the train," I said, "it would be very interesting to stay in a hotel. I could write it up for my Idea Book. And I could write Dolly about it for sure."

"It does look like quite a nice place to stay," Damaris said.

It might have been, but we didn't find out. We didn't stay there. We did miss the train, though.

It was quite some time before we figured out it wasn't just the cotton business that had brought Papa to Sacramento, or what had kept him there. It had to do with money and what Papa called a grubstake.

TWELVE

After we missed the train to San Francisco, Papa said
not to worry. We could finish our trip the next day
in grand style on the Overland Limited instead of
making do with the local.

"In the meantime," he said, "we have to bed you
down somewhere tonight. Not here—it's full to the
rafters—but there's a rooming house nearby."

It wasn't nearby.

It was seven blocks away, which seems longer when
you are carrying practically all you own with you.
Papa didn't carry anything but his cane.

Damaris slowed down, and I dropped back to keep
her company. She was breathing hard. She laces those
corsets she wears too tightly. Papa and Joel didn't
notice. They went briskly on. They have long legs,
flat heels on their shoes, and don't wear corsets.

Finally Papa looked back and said, "Hurry along,
Abigail!" just as though it was *me*, as though it were
I, who was slowing us down!

Damaris and I had to share a bed.

It was an iron double bedstead with a thin mattress and springs that sagged in the middle, so we rolled together all night long. The pillows felt as if they were stuffed with wood, not feathers. The sheets and pillowcases looked clean, though, and there was a bathroom down the hall, so we didn't have to go visit a privy out back.

Unscreened windows opened onto the street, and I decided no one else in Sacramento ever went to sleep. We heard people outside all night long. There wasn't a breath of air. With the noise and the heat and the mosquitoes, it was hard to sleep. I was sure if I turned on a light, something with big eyes and a large sucking proboscis would be staring back at me.

Damaris turned over on her side of our lumpy mattress.

"Are you awake?" I asked.

"Yes."

"About Papa . . ."

"What about Papa?"

I swatted a mosquito.

"He isn't married yet," I said.

"No, he isn't."

"I guess I needn't have worried clear across the country about what to call Mrs. MacKay."

"No," she said.

I stared into the hot darkness.

Another mosquito whined in my ear. I swatted at

it, but, like worries, there always seemed to be another one buzzing around.

At least we'd found Papa.

"He called Mrs. MacKay Molly. It's a comfortable sort of name, isn't it? A good name for an old widow lady. Maybe we can call her Aunt Molly." I started imagining Mrs. MacKay soft and plump with hair beginning to go gray. "I wonder if she has any children. Papa didn't say. . . ."

"Go to sleep, Abby," Damaris said. "There'll be time to talk in the morning."

I curled up and left only my nose sticking out for the mosquitoes to dine on and finally fell asleep.

I woke sticky-eyed and scratching. Damaris was already awake dabbing water on her face at the washstand.

"Hurry up, sleepyhead," she said. "Papa and Joel are waiting downstairs to take us to breakfast. And"—she looked at me critically—"whatever happened to your nose?"

I looked hopelessly in the mirror at the red itchy blob on my face.

"I look awful!"

"Don't scratch," advised Damaris. "Rub some soap on it, and maybe it won't itch so much." She had bites too, but not on her nose.

Joel took one look and said, "Hello, knob nose!"

Papa didn't notice. He took us to a café, where we

ate steak and biscuits and boiled beans. Papa was as elegant as ever and cheerful. He asked us how we had slept but didn't really listen to our answer. Instead he started talking about Nevada, the "land of opportunity."

"Nevada didn't look like any land of opportunity to me," I whispered to Joel. "It was just plain old empty desert."

Papa heard me.

"You think so?" he said.

"That's what it looked like to me."

"You better marry yourself a rich husband, sis." He smiled. His teeth were white as bone under his blond mustache. Papa has very good teeth.

"Why?" I said, thinking, I am not Papa's sister, so why does he call me sis, and I hadn't any intention of ever marrying any husband, rich, poor, or middling! And especially one that was aggravating!

"You aren't ever going to make a fortune on your own, daughter, not if you turn up your nose at opportunity because of a little heat and sand and hard work. They're taking *millions* in silver out of the Nevada mines! Gold too."

Papa's eyes sparkled as though the millions were stacked up on the tablecloth in front of him.

"Whereabouts in Nevada?" Joel said.

"Tonopah," said Papa.

Damaris played with her water glass while Joel and

I looked at each other uneasily. Aunt Eunice used to say Papa had been bit by the mining bug young and never recovered.

About the time we finished breakfast Papa thought to ask about Uncle George and Aunt Eunice but didn't seem much interested in our answers until Damaris said something about Uncle George losing his business.

"Bankrupt?" said Papa.

"Uncle George intends to pay back every cent he owes!" I said.

"Always the honorable man," Papa said in an odd voice. It made me wonder if Papa was a little bit jealous of Uncle George, but, of course, that couldn't be.

He tossed a silver dollar on the table to pay for our breakfasts and marched us briskly off to the railway station. Damaris took his arm to slow him down.

"I'm glad you met us here in Sacramento, Papa," Damaris said. "I was anxious about the big city. We are really country mice. . . ."

"You'll do fine, princess," Papa said. "I'll send a telegram ahead so Molly will expect you."

"Us? You mean . . ." Damaris stopped when a man with a derby hat and smoking a fat cigar hailed Papa.

"Jack Edwards!" he said. "Over here!"

The man's name was Sam Stritch. He had a large fat stomach with a gold watch chain draped across it, little shoe-button black eyes, and a gold front tooth. Papa said Sam might have Gold in his teeth but he had Silver in his heart and that they were partners.

"Let me get my family on the train, Sam, and then we'll talk business," Papa said.

Damaris stopped in her tracks.

"Aren't you coming with us?" she asked.

"Not now, princess." He glanced sideways. The man in the derby hat pointed toward the bar, and Papa nodded.

"But where are you going?" Damaris asked.

"To Tonopah, to make our fortune! To buy baubles for my beautiful daughter . . . daughters," he corrected, looking at me. "A matter I will have to explain to Mrs. MacKay too."

"But what are we to do?" For once Damaris, who always acts so grown-up, looked as though she were going to cry.

"Molly expects you. Expected you yesterday. I'll wire her to meet you."

"But how will we know her? And suppose she doesn't meet us?"

"Then hire a cab," Papa said, sounding impatient. He pulled out his wallet, peeled off some bills, and handed them to Joel.

"See to your sisters," he said, hurrying us off to the station and through the hustle and bustle of people to the platform where the Overland stood hissing and steaming, ready to depart.

Papa hadn't ever intended to come with us, I thought. Whatever he said, he was in town mostly to see that Sam Stritch. . . .

Just then a small form trailing a harness scrambled down the train's boarding steps and darted out into the crowd, slithering under and around legs.

"Buster?" I said.

It was Buster. And he was headed straight for the two-block-long mahogany bar.

Ladies aren't allowed at the bar, but I'm not a lady yet, so I only hesitated maybe half a second before I took off after him. It wasn't a minute too soon.

When I reached him, Buster had already climbed up on the bar and was busy sampling the free lunch and someone's leftover beer.

"Babby!" he said cheerfully, waving a pickled pig's foot at me.

The customers seemed highly entertained. I ignored them, wiped off Buster's hands and his foam mustache, hauled him back to the train, and handed him over to Mrs. Benton, who was scanning the crowd anxiously.

"My dear! How can I thank you?" she said. "Buster darling, are you all right, my pet?"

Buster hiccuped gently.

THIRTEEN

After the commotion died down, Damaris introduced
Papa to Mrs. Benton. Papa took off his hat. Without
it he didn't look a whole lot older than Joel, except
for his mustache.

"Dear lady, I have heard a great deal about you,"
he said. And then he smiled. Papa has really perfect
teeth for a man his age.

"I hope what you've heard is good," said Mrs. Benton.

"Nothing but, dear lady. I must thank you for taking
my children under your wing." Papa didn't say he'd
called her our *warden*. I guess he couldn't and still be
polite.

Buster was sitting on the ground, interestedly picking up paper rings from cigars. He had one stuck on
each finger.

"I'm the one that's grateful, Mr. Edwards." Mrs.
Benton straightened her hat and smiled. "Abby has
been very good with the children."

"Nevertheless, I am grateful. It will ease my mind

for them to have your company on the remainder of their journey."

"But surely you're accompanying them, Mr. Edwards?"

"No, I regret to say," Papa said, but he didn't look one bit regretful to me. He said he was only persuaded to leave us because our financial future and "ultimate welfare" depended on the success of his venture.

Then he said Mrs. MacKay would collect us at the end of the line, which made us sound like parcels wrapped in brown paper and string!

"Does Mrs. MacKay have children?" asked Mrs. Benton.

"Regretfully no," said Papa.

Then he complimented her on her "handsome children," smiled, tipped his hat, and left.

"What a charming man," said Mrs. Benton, but I felt embarrassed. Papa had pushed us off on someone again.

Then the boarding bell sounded and Mrs. Benton scooped Buster up and herded us all on board. We started to wave at Papa, but he had already turned to go.

Damaris and Joel seemed awfully quiet.

"Does Papa lie?" I asked as Joel stowed our satchels in the luggage rack.

"No, of course not," Damaris said.

"About leaving because of our . . . welfare?"

"That's what he really feels."

"Then he's fooling himself, isn't he?"

"Perhaps."

"I'd rather not fool myself," I said. It seems an awful waste of time to fool yourself. Mama used to say, "Always tell the truth. That way you don't have to try to keep your stories straight."

"Look who's here," Joel said, pointing out the window at a tall young lady running across the platform, her skirts and petticoats hiked with one hand and hanging on to her hat with the other.

It was Miss Eleanor.

The porter helped her aboard our car a minute before he hauled up the little boarding step. Miss Eleanor sank into a seat and fanned herself with her hat.

After she caught her breath, Miss Eleanor told us how she'd missed the train the day before. She'd been hunting up the washroom. And she'd almost missed our train too. For the same reason.

"But where did you stay?" I asked.

"I managed quite well," she said.

I finally wormed it out of her. Miss Eleanor sat up all night on one of those hard benches in the station waiting room. She said she'd slept a bit, but I'll bet it wasn't much. Her eyes were all red.

"It was very interesting," she said. "There are some rather unusual people wandering about at night. I felt quite adventurous! I kept expecting something tremendous to happen."

"Did it?" asked Joel.

"No. But it might have." Then she looked past us and, sounding disappointed, said, "Your father . . . he's not with you?"

"No," I said.

"Such a fine-looking man. . . ."

Papa *was* a fine-looking man, and I supposed he did mean well. All the same . . .

I stared out the window at the river, the dry flat land, and the hazy blue of the mountains to the west. I wished I were back home, wished Mama were still alive. . . .

Damaris was quiet, and Joel too. I guess they were thinking about Papa. And about Mrs. MacKay waiting in San Francisco. Mrs. Benton called San Francisco the City and said we must remember never ever to call it Frisco, as that was a dreadful "faux pas" and practically an "Unforgivable Sin."

Miss Eleanor kept brushing her clothes and touching her hair and putting on and taking off her gloves. She found a tiny rip in one of the gloves, probably from putting them on and taking them off so much. Damaris mended it for her.

I think Miss Eleanor's "taking care of herself" muscles had gone to jelly, since she hadn't had to use them, mostly because the Colonel wouldn't let her.

She kept reading a letter she had from Mr. Quentin Jerome and looking at his picture.

"I wonder if Mr. Jerome will recognize me without Daddy being along," Miss Eleanor said.

"Well, you'll recognize him anyway," I said. "From his picture."

"He's good-looking, don't you think, Abby?"

"Yes," I said. He was, except for his eyes, which were a little too close together. "He looks like a . . ." Joel kicked me in the shins right then.

"He looks . . . light-complected," I said, glaring at Joel.

I don't know what on earth he thought I was going to say. That Mr. Jerome looked like a pirate maybe. A light-haired pirate.

Miss Eleanor was going to be his second wife. His first wife died.

It doesn't seem right to me that men have all these wives, but ladies seem to get all tuckered out having big bunches of children and taking care of them and then they die. Like Mama did, though she only had us three.

Then I thought about Mrs. MacKay. Papa was going to be her third husband, so it isn't just gentlemen who get married a lot of times. Mrs. MacKay didn't have bunches of children either. She didn't have any.

I looked over at Buster. I kept waiting for him to do something horrible, but he didn't. Mrs. Benton gave him something she called soothing syrup because his molars were bothering him, and he went to sleep with his thumb in his mouth.

"We live in Berkeley near the university," Philippa

informed me. It's across the Bay from San Francisco. So is Oakland."

"The university is where Papa mostly works," Rose said, "when he's not studying abor . . . abor . . ."

"Aborigines, dear," said Mrs. Benton.

"We can't go back to our own house, though . . ."

"Because Papa sold it," said Philippa.

"Leased it, dear," said Mrs. Benton. "He leased it for the year we'll be gone to the Hawaiian Islands."

"So we're going to our Grandpa Benton's," Rose said.

"And Buster better behave, or Grandpa says he'll tie him to a tree and play Indian with him," Philippa said.

"Indian?" Buster woke up and pressed his nose to the glass. He kept it there as we crossed a narrow neck of water on a train ferry. Then Mrs. Benton said we should get our things together because it wouldn't be long now.

"I don't want you to leave us," said Rose, throwing her arms around me.

"Well, perhaps we can persuade Abby to visit us," said Mrs. Benton.

"Say you will," said Rose.

"If I can."

"That means she probably won't," said Philippa.

"I'll try," I said, giving Rose a hug.

At last the train bumped to a stop at what was

called the Oakland Mole. The Oakland Mole wasn't
an animal that dug holes in the ground, but the place
at the edge of the water where the tracks ended and
the ferries docked.

"End of the line!" called the conductor.

"But surely there's some mistake!" said Miss
Eleanor. "We're supposed to go to San Francisco!"

"You have to take the ferry to the City, miss," the
conductor said.

"I thought you knew, dear," said Mrs. Benton.

I didn't know either. I don't know why people think
you know things just because they do! It's Purely
Aggravating!

Anyway, there we stood on the Oakland Mole,
turning blue. It was June but it was overcast and cold.
The wind off the bay bit right down to the bone, and
nobody met us.

"Where are the palm trees and orange bushes?" I
said, teeth chattering, and wishing for my woolen
winter underdrawers.

"Orange *trees*," said Philippa. "Oranges grow on
trees, not bushes. Oak trees grow in Oakland. That's
why they call it Oakland."

"Thank you for telling me," I said.

"You're welcome," said Philippa as Buster plopped
himself down on the ground and started scooting
around on the seat of his pants.

"Mrs. MacKay probably expects to meet you in the

City," Mrs. Benton said, anxiously scanning the crowd.

No one had yet come for us when Dr. Benton turned up. He was a tall, jolly, cheerful gentleman who swung the girls up in turn, and gave them each a great smacking kiss, even Mrs. Benton.

The soothing syrup had worn off Buster, and he was wriggling at the end of his new harness like a fish on a line. Mrs. Benton kept a firm hold on him and said she was sure we would be all right, but we were to call on her if "anything unforeseen" should happen.

"Come along, Bessie," Dr. Benton said, pulling out a pocket watch about the size of a turnip. (That's an exaggeration. It wasn't quite that big.) "We'll miss the streetcar."

"I don't like to leave you here," Mrs. Benton said.

Just then an extremely large young man with a bushy mustache plowed through the crowd straight toward us. His eye was fixed on Damaris.

"There you are, miss," he said, taking off his hat. "For a minute I thought I'd missed you. . . ."

"Well," Dr. Benton said, "here's their friend come for them. That ought to relieve your mind, Bessie!" He hauled Buster up and heaved him over his shoulder, grabbed a bag with his free hand, and headed for the streetcar.

"But . . ." I started to say.

"Mama, come on!" said Philippa. "We'll lose Papa!"

"Coming, dear. You have our address, Damaris, Joel? And I'll be in touch. . . ." Mrs. Benton kissed us and hurried off after the Professor, who was marching off with Buster dangling over his shoulder and wriggling at both ends.

The young man didn't look twice at me or Joel. He clapped his hat back on, reached for Damaris's valise, and said again, "For a minute I thought I'd missed you, miss."

We didn't know the young man at all.

We didn't know him from Adam's off ox, as Uncle George would have said.

FOURTEEN

"Now, just one minute," Joel said.

Joel is very protective of Damaris, though she doesn't need quite so much taking care of as Joel thinks.

She hung on to her valise and said, "Did Mrs. MacKay send you?"

"Mrs. MacKay? No." The tall young man looked puzzled.

"There's been some mistake, Mr.—" Damaris said.

"Jerome," he said. He didn't look one bit like that picture of Miss Eleanor's! He was a whole lot younger, for one thing. "Aren't you Miss Spencer?"

When Damaris shook her head, he blushed right up to his hat brim and said, "I'm sorry, miss. I'm Nollie. Noland Jerome. I thought you were a little *too* young, though Pa said you'd—that is, she, Miss Spencer, would be young."

"There she is." Damaris pointed toward Miss Eleanor edging her way through the crowd toward us.

"Abby . . . Damaris . . . I'm so glad I didn't lose you!" she said.

"This is Mr. Noland Jerome. I believe he has come for you," Damaris said.

Miss Eleanor peered up uncertainly at Noland's face with its bushy lip ornament.

"Noland?"

"Folks call me Nollie. Pa sent me for you, miss."

"Pa?" said Miss Eleanor, looking alarmed. "Mr. Jerome is . . . your father?"

"I expect you didn't think I'd be so tall. . . ."

Miss Eleanor didn't expect him even to *be*, I thought. I was sure she didn't know Mr. Jerome had any children, much less one the size of a telegraph pole.

"I'm sixteen," Noland said. "Got my growth early. The others are still little shavers."

"The others?" said Miss Eleanor faintly. "How many others are there?"

"Five," said Noland, seizing Miss Eleanor's valise and hoisting it up on his shoulder. "Pa said I was to take good care of you, miss, and show proper respect, you being our new stepma."

"Stepma?" said Miss Eleanor.

I felt very sorry for her. At least Papa had told Mrs. MacKay she was going to be a stepmother.

"Where's the Colonel, miss?"

"In Denver. . . . He had an . . . unfortunate accident. . . ." She didn't explain what the accident was but looked at us and said, "Your father's friend didn't come?"

"No," Damaris said.

"We better get a move on or we'll miss the ferry," Noland said, grabbing up her valise.

"Well, Noland," Miss Eleanor said, "we must see my young friends here safely to their destination."

I thought Noland was going to say something, but instead he just went off to find a cart for Miss Eleanor's luggage.

As she watched him go, Miss Eleanor said, "We must think of all this as *Our Great Adventure!*"

I didn't think it was much of an adventure to feel like country mice marooned in a strange city with nobody to meet you!

And I didn't think finding out you were going to have *six stepchildren*, one of them a great galumphing boy like Noland, was much of an adventure either.

At last Noland came back accompanied by a man with a cart who trundled our luggage along with Miss Eleanor's down the slip and onto the clean scrubbed deck of the ferry. We leaned over the rail to watch the trail of froth stirred up by the paddle wheel as we edged out into the Bay.

Nollie offered to buy us hot coffee (chocolate for me) and "bear claws or snails."

"Bear claws? Snails?" I said, horrified.

"Sweet rolls," he said with a grin. "Not *real* bear claws and snails."

Miss Eleanor took a sip of coffee and then said, "Since my father's not here, Noland, I do not think it entirely suitable that I go to your home. I would like to go to"—she consulted the address Papa had given her—"Mrs. Wheeler's boardinghouse."

"Pa said you were coming home."

"I'll explain to Mr. Jerome. It will be more seemly if I stay elsewhere. I'm sure he will understand."

Nollie shook his head. "Pa gets mighty perturbed if folks don't do what he says exactly and immediate like."

"I'll take the responsibility, Noland." Miss Eleanor's cheeks were pink.

"Pa won't like it much."

"I insist," said Miss Eleanor, which must have been about the first time in her life Miss Eleanor ever insisted on anything!

Nollie stood there still wrinkling up his forehead. Then he said, "I expect you can tell him your own self, miss."

Miss Eleanor made us promise to look her up at Mrs. Wheeler's as soon as we were settled.

If we ever did get settled, I thought.

"Don't worry so, Abby," Miss Eleanor said, patting my hand. "I'm sure everything will be all right. You must call and tell me all the news . . . about your papa . . . and Mrs. MacKay, of course."

When we were stuffed full of snails and bear claws,

Nollie took us out onto the deck. As he slid open the door the wind almost ripped our hats off our heads.

"Wind blows in through the Gate," Nollie said.

"The Gate?" said Damaris.

"The Golden Gate." Nollie pointed to the notch between the hills to the west. "That's the strait, the passage to the ocean. Inside the Gate is the bay. Outside, the whole Pacific Ocean. China, if you go far enough."

"Needs a bridge," said Joel, looking at the narrow slot between the hills with his scientific eye.

"It'll be a while coming," said Nollie. "Water's deep and the currents bad."

Gulls screeched and swooped down on crumbs of bread that passengers tossed to them, catching the bits before they ever hit the water. Up ahead were the hills of San Francisco and the clock tower of the Ferry Building.

Bells jangled. The ferry slowed and bumped gently into the pilings as it edged into the slip and was made fast. The air smelled of salt and of the creosote used to preserve the wood pilings where the gulls perched, fierce-eyed and glaring.

"What do you suppose Mrs. MacKay looks like?" I said as we made our way into the crowded Ferry Building. My stomach was doing flip-flops, either from the bear claws or from thinking about Mrs. MacKay.

"She's a mighty well set up lady," Nollie said.

"You know her?"

"Pa does, but . . ." He scanned the crowd in the enormous high-ceilinged waiting room. "I don't see her. People can always spot Mrs. MacKay by her hair."

"Her hair?"

"Red," said Noland.

But there was no red-haired lady among the waiting crowd.

There was, however, Mr. Quentin Jerome.

He didn't look a bit like Miss Eleanor's picture either. He was older, wore a beard, and was two inches shorter than Noland. When he raised his hat, you could see he didn't have much hair on top of his head, but I figured if you're as old as Miss Eleanor, maybe you don't mind about hair.

When Miss Eleanor told him no one had met us, he frowned. Then he unsnapped his purse (I never saw a man carry a purse before), handed Nollie a dollar, and told him to hire a horse cab and take us out to Mrs. MacKay's.

"Bring back the change," he said, "and see you don't lollygag, boy."

He hustled Miss Eleanor into a buggy. I heard her mention Mrs. Wheeler just before he lifted his whip and laid it smartly on the horse.

Damaris looked doubtfully at the cab Nollie found and the horses pulling it. They surely must have been the poorest, skinniest, most swaybacked nags in the whole city.

"Are you sure they will get us there, Noland?" she asked.

"Sure," he said, though they didn't look like they could make it around the block.

In between thinking about Mrs. MacKay and wondering how we missed her, I kept looking at our poor skinny horses, thinking one of them might keel over and die going up one of the steep hills that poke up from the flatland near the Bay. (They didn't.)

We drove past whole streets of tall wooden houses, mostly painted gray, stuck together smack up against each other with no side yards and no front yards either.

Mrs. MacKay's house was on a smallish hill with a splendid view. The sun was coming out, and the water had turned a greenish blue with an icing of whitecaps. Mrs. MacKay's house wasn't stuck to its neighbor but had a front garden and side yards. It was bigger than Mr. Buttchenbacher's house back in Estes.

We just sat there for a minute looking at the marble steps and gingerbread turrets.

"Mighty grand," said Joel.

"Like something out of a fairy tale," I said. Then I shivered. The wind off the Bay had a bite to it.

Nollie and Joel leaped down and helped unload our luggage. Nollie went all red when Damaris thanked him and said it was nothing and that he hoped we'd see each other again. Of course, he was looking at Damaris when he said it. Then he said he'd best leave, or his pa would have his skin.

"Pa don't take kindly to being crossed, and he's right handy with a quirt."

After he left, Joel said a quirt was a riding whip and Mr. Jerome must have beat the stuffing out of Noland when he was little, or he wouldn't be so scared of him still.

"At least Papa never beat us," Damaris said.

"Wasn't around long enough to," Joel said as we walked up the marble steps.

He pulled on the bell. It echoed in back of the house, and then we heard the shuffle of footsteps and the door opened.

A Chinese gentleman wearing white pajamas stood there. A queue of shiny black hair braided into a pigtail hung down his back.

I was most astonished, since I had never seen a Chinese gentleman before, except in a stereopticon picture. I decided at once I'd best not write Uncle George and Aunt Eunice about him. I knew Aunt Eunice would surely send us warnings about opium dens and white slavers.

"We would like to see Mrs. MacKay," Damaris said.

"Missee not home."

Not home! Didn't she expect us? My heart sank

down to my toenails, but Damaris straightened up as though she had a steel rod running up the back of her corset.

"We'll wait," she said.

Then she marched right past Charlie—that's the name of the Chinese gentleman—with her chin in the air, straight into Mrs. MacKay's front parlor, with Joel and me trailing along behind.

She sat down on one plush upholstered chair next to a green-marble fireplace. Joel took the other chair, and I plumped myself down on the sofa, which was not as comfortable as it looked, being stuffed with horsehair.

"We might get him in trouble," I said.

"Who?" said Damaris, as though her mind were a couple million miles away.

"The Chinese gentleman."

"Houseboy," said Joel. "That's what they're called."

"Houseboy?" That did not sound right to me, since he was an older gentleman. "Whatever he's called, he might get into trouble letting us in when Mrs. MacKay isn't here."

"What else were we to do? Sit on the stoop until she comes home? There's obviously been some mix-up. Papa said she would expect us."

"But did Papa tell *her* to expect us? Or did he tell someone else?" I asked.

"He said he'd send a wire."

"But did he?"

"Of course he did!"

Joel and I just looked at each other. Joel shrugged.

Damaris said, "Papa wouldn't just foist us off on someone without their permission!"

FIFTEEN

Mrs. MacKay's parlor was extremely elegant.

There wasn't a speck of dust anywhere, and the polished floors and furniture smelled of beeswax and turpentine. I sat very gingerly on the sofa so as not to leave a dent in the upholstery. Damaris and Joel looked stiff as boards.

Mrs. MacKay's full-length portrait hung over the marble fireplace. I supposed it was Mrs. MacKay's portrait, and it turned out it was.

I looked at the picture once and then tried not to, but my eyes kept sliding back as though they had a mind of their own. There was quite a lot of Mrs. MacKay to see. She was dressed in a satin and lace ball gown, at least part of her was. There was an awful lot of Mrs. MacKay's bare-skin front showing. Damaris called it décolletage. Whatever it was, Joel's eyes kept sliding back to it too.

In the street a carriage clattered down the hill toward the Bay, the sound muffled by the velvet drapes at the windows.

"All we do lately is wait!" I said, impatiently jumping up and almost crashing into the Chinese gentleman, which would have made an awful mess, as he was carrying a tray of tea and cookies.

"You Mr. Edwards's kiddies?" he said.

"Yes," said Damaris.

"Not little kiddies. Big," he said, grinning, which I thought was rather rude of him.

"Charlie meet train yesterday. Not find kiddies."

"We were delayed," Damaris said.

"By a wreck," Joel explained.

"Ah, very bad," Charlie clucked sympathetically, and left us to drink our tea. After that I took out my Idea Book and sketched the room so I wouldn't forget it. Joel went to sleep sitting up. He said he was just going to rest his eyes, but he surely looked asleep to me. Damaris sat with her hands clasped on her lap.

The clock on the mantel had just chimed four-thirty when we heard the click of heels on the front steps and a sharp pull on the bell.

"Good afternoon, Charlie," a woman said. "I forgot my key. Is Mr. Edwards back yet?"

"No, Missee MacKay. Telegram come. Kiddies here."

"Kiddies?"

"In parlor, missee."

In novels ladies are always *sweeping* into rooms (it sounds as though they are trailing brooms), but Mrs. MacKay did sweep into the room, skirts swishing, and smelling of violets. She does have red hair, the shade Aunt Eunice used to say comes in a packet of henna.

We stood up when she came into the room. That's what Mama, and Aunt Eunice too, taught us to do when our elders enter the room, only Mrs. MacKay doesn't look *extremely* elderly.

She is not very tall, but that hasn't stopped her from what Aunt Eunice calls blossoming. She blossoms above and below the waist, so I think she must have a mighty powerful corset. It isn't a bit natural or healthy to have such a squished-in middle, if you ask me, though, of course, it is extremely fashionable.

"Well, here you are," she said as she looked us up and down, wrinkling her nose a tiny bit as though we smelled of the train, which I expect we did. We'd had to sleep in our traveling clothes on the train and hadn't had an all-over bath since we left Kansas. We'd sponged ourselves off every day. At least Damaris and I had. I don't know what Joel did, but it is purely impossible to wash *all over* in a train washroom.

"And where is your father?"

"Papa? Why, he's in Tonopah. . . ."

"Tonopah? What's he doing there? He was just supposed to check on a cotton order. . . ."

"I don't know anything about that," Damaris said as the Chinese man came in with a yellow envelope in his hand.

"Telegram, missee," he said.

"Thank you, Charlie."

Mrs. MacKay ripped open the envelope and scanned the lines; then she laughed, though somehow she didn't sound as if she thought anything was very funny.

"It is from your father, rather late to announce your arrival. He says, 'Opportunity knocks.' He should have said, 'Silver calls.' "

Damaris and Joel and I looked at one another. We knew how it was with Papa, all right, when silver called. Or gold. Or copper.

"He's found a backer with development money who is interested in a new mining prospect. How like John. . . . And how like him not to tell me. . . ." She looked back and forth between us and left the sentence dangling in the air. What hadn't he told her? I wondered. Was it about us?

Mrs. MacKay had written Uncle George that she would be happy to meet us. Maybe, I thought, she'd meant years in the future. Maybe she hadn't necessarily meant she would be glad to have us *live* with her. It must be entirely upsetting to have the three of us arrive on her doorstep without Papa.

"Well, something, I suppose, must be done with you," she said. "I daresay it's up to me."

"I'm sorry we were late," Damaris said, her chin going up, "but you did expect us. . . ."

"Yes," she said, but I was sure there was something she didn't expect.

She tapped her small foot in its gray kid shoe on

the floor. Then she said, "I have an engagement this evening, but Charlie will see to your beds and your dinner."

Damaris nodded. She looked very pale. Joel glanced at her. Then he said, "Thank you, Mrs. MacKay."

"Call me Molly," she said, smiling suddenly.

That was Most Astonishing!

Aunt Eunice would about skin us alive if we called a grown-up person by her first name. She said it didn't show proper respect. Mama said so too. She and Aunt Eunice mostly never even called their friends by their first names. Mrs. Raymond, Dolly's ma, didn't even call her *husband* by his first name.

"It's Molly, remember," she said, tapping Joel on the cheek. "You're as handsome as your father."

Joel turned red, tomato red, a ripe tomato red. He was still red when Charlie, his queue bobbing back and forth behind him, led us upstairs to our rooms.

Damaris and I had a bedroom on the third floor with an adjoining sitting room that looked out over the back garden. I opened the window and turned up my nose at the smell.

"Eucalyptus tree. Smell good," Charlie said, but it reminded me of the liniment Mama rubbed on our chests when we had colds. Or of the medicines in Colonel Spencer's sample case.

Joel had a room just below us, next to the bathroom. The bathroom was about as large as his room and equipped with a huge enameled iron tub set on claw feet. After Mrs. MacKay left, we all took turns in the tub and scrubbed off *tons* of train dirt.

I told Joel, "You look like you took off a layer of skin along with the dirt!"

Then he said, "You're as pink as Buster Benton's bottom yourself," which was a Purely Horrible thing for him to say!

Damaris and I went to find something for supper in the kitchen. We had no sooner poked our nose through the door when the cook (not Charlie) screeched at us in Chinese, which, of course, we didn't understand. When we didn't move, he picked up a cleaver and waved it in the air, so we backed out *very quickly.*

The cook's name was Ah Sing. Charlie's name is really Lu Chang, though here in San Francisco he is just called Charlie. He said back in China where he comes from they call California the Gold Mountain, but that he hadn't found any gold yet.

Charlie told us to wait in the back parlor and he would bring in our dinner. Back home in Estes we would call it supper, but Charlie called it dinner.

The back parlor looked out on the garden. It had comfortable chairs, houseplants, and a library table piled with magazines, and it was much cozier than the front parlor. There was even a cat with a jeweled necklace curled up on the most comfortable chair.

"Cat called Sapphire," said Charlie.

Sapphire opened one eye and looked at us, then stretched and stalked out of the room, nose in the air.

"Cat not like strangers," said Charlie.

Us, I thought. It took after Mrs. MacKay.

Charlie brought us lamb chops and new potatoes, baby carrots and cheese and pickles, a summer salad, and for dessert, chocolate éclairs. Ah Sing had a terrible temper, but he was a good cook.

I quite enjoyed my dinner, but Damaris just picked at her food. I knew she was thinking about Papa and Mrs. MacKay. Then I wasn't so hungry anymore either, but it didn't bother Joel. He ate until you'd think he'd about burst.

Then he leaned back and said, "A man could get spoiled."

"Man, pooh!" I said.

"What do you think?" Damaris said, as though she hadn't heard a word we said.

"About what?" Joel said.

"Mrs. MacKay."

"She is beautiful," Joel said.

"Not as beautiful as Mama!" I said, glaring at him.

"You needn't go up like a firecracker, Abby," he said, which reminded me of my birthday, which is next month, though I expect nobody else will remember it.

"Well, she's not as beautiful as Mama would have

been if she had pearls and fancy gowns to wear and had a houseboy and cook to do all the work!" I said.

"Nobody could be like Mama, Abby," Joel said.

"Mrs. MacKay didn't like us," said Damaris.

"She liked Joel," I said.

"Of course," said Joel. "How could she help it?" I slung one of Mrs. MacKay's embroidered pillows at him and hit the library table, knocking off some of the magazines.

"Now you've done it!" said Joel.

"Have not!" I bent down to pick them up. For a minute I just knelt there looking at a batch of school brochures among the magazines, brochures for boarding schools for children six to twelve.

"What have you found, Abby?" Joel asked.

I held out the catalogues. One was for a military school, several for young ladies' finishing schools, a couple for younger girls.

"She didn't know how old we were," I said. "Papa didn't tell her."

"He must have!" Damaris said.

"He probably forgot. You know he never remembers our birthdays, except yours, Damaris, sometimes. Mrs. MacKay thought we'd be little. . . ."

"And not much trouble," said Joel, "especially if we were packed off to boarding schools."

"Separate schools. Why, we wouldn't even see each other!"

Mama always told us to remember we were a family and to watch out for one another. How could we do that if we were off at different boarding schools?

"Mama wouldn't like it," Damaris said.

"Well, it hasn't happened yet, so no need to pucker your brow," Joel said.

Then he belched, which was rude, and said he was full as a tick, which sounded rude too. Damaris gave him Aunt Eunice's lecture on politeness. For a while it took her mind off whatever she had been thinking, which was probably why he did it.

Mrs. MacKay wasn't back when we went up to bed. I watched Damaris take down her hair. It shimmered like gold. I wished mine did.

"Mrs. MacKay was awfully upset, Papa not being here."

"Yes," Damaris said as she turned off the light.

"At least, she knew there were going to be three of us. Poor Miss Eleanor didn't know Mr. Jerome had any children at all!"

I sank into the soft mattress. I didn't think I would go right off to sleep, since I had so much to think about. It did feel Purely Marvelous to be in a real bed with down pillows and feather-light quilts after sleeping sitting up on the train or with Damaris in that lumpy bed in Sacramento.

Suddenly I heard this awful deep groan and moan.

"What's that?" I said, sitting straight up in bed and clutching the quilt around me.

"A foghorn, I think," Damaris said. "To warn ships in the Bay."

"Are you sure? It sounds like an ogre with the stomachache."

The foghorn groaned again, and then I heard the clink of horseshoes on the cobblestoned street and a carriage stop in front of the house. I hopped out of bed and went to peek out the window. Damaris did too.

The gaslights were ringed with fog but gave enough light so we could see Mrs. MacKay's red hair and the glitter of her jewels as she got out of the carriage. Then the front door opened and closed. I heard Mrs. MacKay laugh and a man's voice.

"Papa?" I whispered, though it didn't exactly sound like Papa.

"No," said Damaris. She was right. It wasn't.

SIXTEEN

"It's not Papa," Damaris *said again, but I didn't be-*
lieve her.

I went dashing out to the top of the stairs, where
Damaris pulled me to a stop.

"Listen!" she said.

A man's voice floated up from the front hall. It
wasn't Papa's.

"My dear Molly," he said, "I advise you to be very
careful if you insist on marrying this dirty-fingered
miner of yours, or you may wind up without a dime
to your name."

Mrs. MacKay said Papa wasn't dirty-fingered.

"A figure of speech. I'm sure the man must have
great charm to have won your affections. . . ."

Mrs. MacKay said Papa not only had clean fingers
but also had been very helpful and considerate when
Mr. MacKay died.

"Ah, that explains it, but you know there are any
number of fellows willing and able to help a grieving
young widow."

Mrs. MacKay laughed and asked if he was volunteering.

"It's possible. However, if you have your heart set on your miner, I advise you to see a lawyer to make sure your property remains yours."

"I have."

"Has the miner agreed?"

"He will."

The man laughed and said he should have known Mrs. MacKay wouldn't lose her head with her heart. Then they went into the back parlor, and Damaris and I went back to bed.

It was hard to go to sleep listening to the sound of the foghorn. I thought about sailors lost in the fog. And about us. And about Papa. What if Papa never came back? What would we do? We couldn't keep on living with Mrs. MacKay.

Morning came at last. It was cold. Not like summer at all. In the next few days, we discovered that at night fog poured in from the ocean through the Golden Gate. By afternoon the wind usually blew away the fog, and it was sunny and bright though not always warm.

We didn't see a whole lot of Mrs. MacKay. She went to work early and visited friends in the evenings. She seemed to have a great many friends, not just gentlemen friends.

On Sunday when Damaris made us put on our best clothes to go to church, she noticed Joel's legs sticking way out beyond his pant legs. She frowned and said Monday he'd best go buy some new pants, especially if . . .

"If what?" I said.

"Just *if.*"

"If I go to work and become a big tycoon and make bushels of money and wear a gold watch," Joel said.

"You're too skinny. You'll have to grow more stomach if you're going to be a tycoon," I said.

"I suppose there's nothing to be done now," Damaris said, looking at Joel's socks and anklebones poking out from his pant legs (not his stomach).

"I'll scrunch down so nobody will notice," Joel said.

It felt strange going to a church where we didn't know anybody at all.

Monday the fog lifted early. It looked to be a wonderful day. And, of course, I had to come down sick!

Joel poked his head around the door, took a look at me, and said I had a bad case of "homesickitis" and that I probably wouldn't die from it, as hardly anyone ever does, but if I did, they would write me up in the medical journals.

"Homesickitis?" said Damaris. "There's no such word."

"If it's not that," said Joel, "it was too much apple pie last night."

"You should talk! Joel Edwards, the champion pie eater of all time!"

Damaris told me to stay in bed until my stomach settled and then ask Ah Sing for some tea and toast.

"I can't!" I said. I *wailed* actually.

"Why not?"

"He'll throw that cleaver at me!"

Ah Sing still wouldn't let Damaris and me anywhere near the kitchen, but he had taken a liking to Joel and gave him lichee nuts and bits of candied ginger.

"Ask Charlie, or get Joel to do it now," Damaris said.

"Not me," said Joel.

"Not I," Damaris corrected.

I don't think California is good for Damaris's character. She is becoming awfully schoolmarmy!

"Where are you going?" I asked as she tucked her hair under her hat. Damaris has little blond tendrils at her neck and forehead, which look pretty on her. On me it would just look messy.

"Downtown to see Dr. Merrick."

Well, I had to sit straight up in bed then, even if my stomach flipped right over and turned to green liver!

"Dr. Viola Merrick? The lady doctor who patched up Colonel Spencer on the train?"

"The same."

"Are you sick too, Damaris?"

"No."

"Then why are you going?"

"To ask for a job. Joel and I . . . we don't like imposing on Mrs. MacKay. . . ."

"I knew it!" I said.

They had figured it out behind my back. They were both going to look for work. That's why Damaris had made such a fuss about Joel's pants. They must be worrying about Papa not coming back too.

"And I'll put in an application at an insurance company. I've heard they're hiring typewriter girls."

"Is Joel going to be a typewriter girl too?"

Joel made as though to punch me in the arm, but didn't. He said he had to take it easy on his "poor sickly baby sister." Then he said he was going to see about a job down at the power company.

"After you get new pants!" said Damaris.

"If I can't get on at the power company, I'll run errands, deliver groceries, or sell newspapers. I won't need new pants for that!"

"Well," I said, "I'm not going to be the only one sitting around not doing anything! I can always go to work as a mother's help. I have *lots* of experience!"

"Not until you feel better," Damaris said.

"Wouldn't make too good an impression to throw up all over your future employer, Abby," Joel said. "Besides, who do you know here who would hire you?"

"Mrs. Benton, that's who!"

"Wait until you're sure you're all right, Abby," Damaris said.

"Think about Buster." Joel grinned. "Just be a lazy slugabed bird waiting for us to bring you home a nice fat worm!"

Joel is full of Perfectly Disgusting ideas!

"You can write to Aunt Eunice and Uncle George while we're gone," Damaris said. "But don't put in anything that will worry them. Or anything that could be food for gossip."

"So what shall I write?" I said.

"Tell the truth," Damaris said. "Papa is away on business. Mrs. MacKay has been pleasant to us."

"And that they aren't married yet?"

"If you say Mrs. MacKay, I think they'll know."

"You don't need to write a twenty-volume encyclopedia, Abby," Joel said. "Just let the folks know we got here all right and are still alive."

"I don't have any stamps."

"Get three," Joel said, tossing me a dime.

I did begin to feel better after they left, so I went downstairs, and Charlie said he would bring "Little Miss" (that's me) breakfast.

Mrs. MacKay had already gone to her business, the Travers Cotton Mill, which she inherited from her husband. Her first husband. She inherited the house from her second. Papa would be her third.

Imagine having three husbands! I probably won't ever have one, being so thin and skinny, which is all right, as I don't want one anyway. Aunt Eunice always said I would change my mind about that, but I haven't so far.

I could hear Ah Sing banging pots and kettles in the kitchen.

Joel says Ah Sing and Charlie mostly eat rice and noodles. Mrs. MacKay doesn't *make* them eat rice and noodles. Ah Sing cooks all these other things for Mrs. MacKay, but he'd rather have his rice or noodles with a few bits of vegetables and meat or fish, which I guess he likes better.

I did wonder where Charlie and Ah Sing slept. Then I found out. They had rooms down in the basement along with the laundry tubs, not that they did the laundry. Another Chinese gentleman they call a wash boy comes in once a week to do it.

Both Charlie and Ah Sing wore white pajamas when they were working, but on their days off they wore regular black suits with skinny-legged trousers, shirts with celluloid collars, and splendid derby hats. Joel said they were saving money to go back to China and get married, but it might be a long time before they could, as they kept spending their salary on the fan-tan games in Chinatown. Fan-tan is a gambling game.

Charlie asked what I would like for breakfast. Then he looked at me and said, "Little Miss is sad. Maybe homesickly."

Charlie speaks very good English, though sometimes

his words sound a little strange. I do not think "home-sickly" is a proper word. I must remember to look it up in the dictionary. Of course, Joel said "homesick-itis," and I don't think that's a proper word either.

"Don't you ever get homesick, Charlie?" I asked. Then I thought about his playing the fan-tan games and not being able to save money to go back to China to get married, and I thought, There I go saying the wrong thing again.

Charlie didn't seem upset, though. He said, "There is old saying, Little Miss."

"What?"

"Best not to let birds of sadness make nests in your hair. Best you find something to do, Little Miss."

"I could cook my own breakfast," I said, wondering why everybody in this whole entire world had advice to give me.

"Best not to do that, Little Miss."

"I expect not," I said with another sigh. "I'd better keep my nose out of the kitchen unless I want Ah Sing's cleaver in my skull bone."

After my breakfast of eggs and hotcakes, I did finally write the letter. I didn't know whether to write Aunt Eunice and Uncle George about Charlie and Ah Sing or not. I thought at least I'd best not mention fan-tan or Ah Sing's cleaver.

I wrote, "Dear Aunt Eunice and Uncle George: We are fine and hope you are the same."

It was a quite terribly boring letter, with all the

interesting parts that might be food for gossip or worry left out. After I chewed on my pen awhile I put in that maybe they could come out to California and open a boardinghouse, seeing as how Aunt Eunice was a pretty good cook.

Then I tied my dime in my handkerchief so I wouldn't lose it and went out to buy stamps. The sun had come out, and the Bay was blue as ink with little crispy whitecaps.

I walked along the waterfront (the street is called the Embarcadero) and went clear out to Fisherman's Wharf, where men were unloading crabs. I like to look at the fishing boats and listen to fishermen talk Italian. I guess it is Italian, as they mostly are.

The water smelled of salt and fish and made little slapping noises against the wooden piers. I thought about the time I fell in the lake and Papa pulled me out so I didn't drown. He must have liked me then, to pull me out.

A cable car came clanging along behind me as I climbed the hill back toward the house. I stopped to watch it, because we didn't have cable cars back in Estes, Kansas, and that would be something to write Aunt Eunice and Uncle George about that surely couldn't be a cause for worry, or gossip either.

The cable cars have a closed section at one end and open-air seats at the other. The seats face the street, so it's easy for people to hop on or off. A young lady was sitting in one of the open-air seats.

She reminded me of Miss Eleanor.

I wondered if Miss Eleanor had married Mr. Jerome yet and if the Colonel had recovered from his wound. That's what I'll do, I thought. I'll go see Miss Eleanor.

I went back to the house and hunted up the address of Mrs. Wheeler's boardinghouse, but I had to ask Charlie how to get there.

"You have car fares, Little Miss?" he asked.

"No, I can walk."

"Long walk. Best take trolley. You take dime."

"I don't know when I can pay you back."

"No need, Little Miss."

Charlie, I decided, was a very nice person, but if people did not pay him back, how would he ever be able to go back to China and get married?

I would be sure to pay him back, though, I thought, even (sigh) if it meant taking care of Buster Benton!

SEVENTEEN

Mrs. Wheeler's house was tall and skinny, and built smack-dab up against its neighbor with no front yard, or side yard either.

Miss Eleanor herself answered the bell.

"Abby, dear!" she said, kissing both my cheeks. She had her hat on and was on her way downtown to buy cigars for the Colonel. She asked me to keep her company.

"The Colonel's here?" I asked.

"Yes, indeed. Poor Daddy. He is still in a good deal of pain. . . ."

As we walked down the hill toward the trolley, Miss Eleanor almost lost her hat in the wind. If she had, it would have sailed straight on down to the crab boats tied up at the Embarcadero. She hung on, though, and said she was going to have to get a smaller hat that would stay on better.

"Or stronger hatpins," I said.

She said they didn't come any stronger. Then she

started asking how we all were and how we liked Mrs. MacKay.

"All right," I said.

I didn't feel comfortable talking about Mrs. MacKay or Papa, so to change the subject I asked about Noland and Mr. Jerome. Then it was Miss Eleanor's turn to look uncomfortable. She said Noland was fine and she'd met the other children.

"Now that the Colonel's here, I expect you'll be having the wedding soon," I said.

"Hmm," she said.

I couldn't figure out if that was "yes" or "no."

Then she started talking very fast about the food at Mrs. Wheeler's boardinghouse, which wasn't much in her opinion. She shook her head and said she hated to think what her friend Chef Francis would say about it, especially the desserts, which ran to stewed prunes and lumpy puddings.

At the tobacco shop Miss Eleanor took considerable time asking advice about the Colonel's cigars.

"I do hope Daddy likes my selection," she said when we finally finished. Next to the tobacco shop was a harness shop.

"That reminds me," she said, looking in the display of harnesses (for horses). "I had lunch with Mrs. Benton last Saturday. She wants to talk to your father. She would like your help with the children, especially Buster, but now that you have your daddy to take care of you, I don't suppose you need that sort of job. . . ."

"Oh, but I do," I said. (Though not too awfully enthusiastically.)

"I wish I could find employment myself," she said as a wagon came rattling down the street toward us.

"Oh, my!" said Miss Eleanor, yanking at my arm. "We must go in here!" She ducked into the nearest doorway and pulled me in after her.

It was a men's haberdashery.

"Why, it's Noland," I said, peeking out the window from behind the display of men's furnishings. "And Mr. Jerome."

"I daresay," said Miss Eleanor, keeping her eyes glued to the handkerchiefs and suspenders.

"But . . ." I was going to ask if she didn't want to see them, but I stopped in time, for once keeping my mouth shut, though I almost choked doing it.

As soon as the wagon had clattered around the corner, Miss Eleanor told the hovering salesman, "Thank you very much, but we're just looking," and we left.

"You will come back for tea, won't you, Abby? Do you have to let anybody know? Mrs. Wheeler has a telephone, though I confess I haven't learned how to use it."

"No." I shook my head as we heard the clang of a trolley behind us.

"Come along, then!" she said.

We picked up our skirts and raced to the corner to catch the car, and Miss Eleanor almost lost her hat again.

"You're sure your daddy won't worry, Abby?" she said as she dropped our fares in the box.

"Papa's not back."

"Not back?"

"From Tonopah."

"So he's still off adventuring! How fabulously exciting!"

"Do you think so?"

"Of course!" said Miss Eleanor. "Wouldn't you like to be with him?"

"Well, yes, I guess so."

"Some people have all the luck!" said Miss Eleanor.

She pointed out the mansions built by silver kings and railroad barons and said, "When your daddy makes his fortune, you'll probably have a house up there on Nob Hill with the rest of the nabobs!"

"Nabobs?"

"People who strike it rich! Wouldn't that be grand?"

She continued talking, but I wasn't listening.

I was daydreaming about Papa picking silver up in big chunks off the ground and us being "nabobs" and building a mansion up on Nob Hill.

Miss Eleanor said Mrs. Wheeler calls her board-

inghouse a guesthouse, because that sounds more elegant, and she calls her boarders guests.

"*Paying* guests," Miss Eleanor said with a frown,
and I wondered if she and the Colonel were having
trouble with the "paying" part of it.

As we went up the front steps, Miss Eleanor said,
"Mrs. Wheeler is an admirable woman, though Daddy
wouldn't approve if he knew. . . ."

"Knew what?"

"She was on the stage and performed at the mining
camps when she was young. Don't mention it to
Daddy."

"All right," I said. I wondered if Mrs. Wheeler had
worn spangled tights and danced on the tops of bars
for silver dollars.

We met Mrs. Wheeler in the hall.

What a disappointment! She was just an ordinary
old lady with her hair pulled back in a bun and a wart
on her nose.

She said she knew Papa. In fact, she seemed to know
all about Papa. She said he was a "darling boy" and
asked if Molly MacKay was going to "unbuckle her
money belt" and give Papa his "stake."

"Steak?" I said. (The English language is sometimes
very confusing!) "Oh, Mrs. MacKay gives us all plenty
to eat. . . ."

"Grubstake," said Mrs. Wheeler. "Mining money.
Not cow meat. Is she going to finance your pa's mine?"

"I don't know," I said. "I don't think he's got a mine yet. I think he's looking for one."

"If I were Molly MacKay," said Mrs. Wheeler, "I'd sell every blessed stick and stitch I owned and go with your pa. . . ." She gave an enormous sigh. "Me and the old man went prospecting ourselves years ago. Those were the days. . . .

"If I had an extra two bits to my name, I'd give it to your pa myself, though I guess if my hubby could tell me (which he can't, being taken to the Good Lord two years ago), he'd say if I had any spare change, I ought to hire me a cook. Never was much good with a skillet. A kitchen is a mighty doleful place, but I'd best get back to it," she said, turning to leave.

Miss Eleanor showed me into the parlor while she went for tea. It was furnished with two armchairs and a sofa and had one potted fern in the sunny bay window. A crocheted doily was pinned to the back of each seat to keep the gentlemen's hair oil from spoiling the upholstery.

The tea was all right, hot and strong, but the milk was blue, and the muffin was more like a pincushion stuffed with sawdust than a muffin.

"Mrs. Wheeler didn't keep paying guests until her husband became ill," Miss Eleanor said.

"Does she have many boarders?" I asked, putting the muffin down.

"No, but her rates are quite reasonable."

"Cheap," said the Colonel, clumping in and sitting down with a groan.

"How are you, Colonel?" I asked politely.

"Tolerable," he said. "Just tolerable. Did you remember my cigars, daughter?"

"Of course, Daddy," she said.

"What's this?" he said, looking at the packet she gave him as though it smelled of skunk. "Where are my Rosa Perfectos?"

"The man at the cigar store said these were just as good and more reasonably priced."

"Cheap!"

Miss Eleanor's cheeks got red, but she didn't offer to go back for Rosa Perfectos. She just said, "Tea, Daddy?"

"What else? You aren't serving champagne, so's I notice!"

He drank his tea silently, glaring at Miss Eleanor, and then stomped upstairs (if you can stomp with a limp), leaving his cigars behind.

"I guess the Colonel's . . . hip . . . is still bothering him," I said, although that was not *exactly* where the Colonel was wounded.

"I'm afraid his temper is my fault," said Miss Eleanor.

"It was Buster Benton who shot him!"

"Daddy thinks all our problems would be solved if only I married Mr. Jerome," she said just as the Colonel clumped back in.

"They would," he said, picking up the cigars. His mustache twitched as he glared at Miss Eleanor.

"I won't marry Mr. Jerome, Daddy. I'd rather starve!"

"You're likely to!"

"Please, Daddy, don't . . ." said Miss Eleanor with a glance at me. She probably felt the same way Aunt Eunice does about telling people family business, but the Colonel paid no attention.

"Five years! We'll both be stone dead of starvation unless you come down from your high horse and marry Jerome. Fool way for your grandmother to tie up your inheritance!"

"What's wrong with Mr. Jerome?" I asked, which I probably shouldn't have.

"Nothing . . ." said Miss Eleanor.

"I'll tell you what! Miss Sparkling Personality here says he's boring. Not interesting enough for her! It's this climate. It's turned the girl pigheaded. . . ."

The Colonel glared at her again and then gathered up his cigars and left.

"We do need money," said Miss Eleanor as the door slammed after him. "I don't know how we're to pay Mrs. Wheeler. Perhaps I *will* have to marry Mr. Jerome."

"Is it the children you don't like, Miss Eleanor?"

"Oh, no. Noland is a dear boy, and the younger ones are quite sweet, really. None of them is as young as Buster Benton. I wouldn't care to undertake a child that age. Daddy's right in a way. I guess it is quite wicked of me. Mr. Jerome is, I'm sure, an admirable man . . . but . . . well"—she blushed—"I did think there ought to be something more. . . ."

I remembered those books Dolly and Mary Margaret Vincent liked to read. *Orange Blossoms and Thorns* and such. That's what Miss Eleanor wants, I thought. *Romance.*

I absentmindedly took a bite of the muffin. It was a mistake, but I couldn't spit it out. It scratched on the way down my throat, so I washed it down with tea.

"Awful, isn't it?" she said.

"Miss Eleanor," I said, "does Mrs. Wheeler have many paying guests?"

"No. As a matter of fact, she doesn't."

"I'll bet it's because of the food."

"It could be."

"Didn't you say Chef Francis taught you how to cook?"

"Yes. Mostly breads and pastries."

"Why don't you see if you could cook in exchange for your room and board?"

"Why, Abby," said Miss Eleanor, "perhaps I could."

"Then you wouldn't have to marry anybody unless you wanted to. . . . There's only one thing, though," I said, looking at her long elegant fingers. "There's bound to be a lot of washing up, pots and such."

"A boy comes to do the washing up. . . ." She looked thoughtful. "I do believe I will discuss the matter with Mrs. Wheeler."

You know how a plant that's getting sort of shriveled in hot dry weather perks up with watering? That's how Miss Eleanor looked. All perked up.

She wouldn't let me go back to Mrs. MacKay's by myself. She pinned her hat back on and said she didn't want me to lose my way. I think she wanted to see the house.

Miss Eleanor's hat almost came to a very sad end.

It would have except for me, Abigail Edwards, Hat Rescuer.

We had gotten off the trolley and were almost at Mrs. MacKay's when the wind scooped that hat right off Miss Eleanor's head. It sailed out into the middle of the street, ribbons flying. I chased after it and snatched it up from in front of a horse cab just as the horse was about to plant a large hoof in its crown.

A man yanked me (and the hat) out of the way and said, "You almost got a hoof in *your* crown that time, chicken!"

"Papa!" I said, throwing my arms around him.

"Take it easy, Abby," he said.

I looked up at him, but he wasn't looking at me. He was smiling at Miss Eleanor.

EIGHTEEN

Miss Eleanor had to look up at Papa, though she is so tall for a lady. Papa gave her that look that turns ladies to mush, and she went all pink and silly.

She reminded me of Dolly and Mary Margaret Vincent talking to boys back home in Estes, but Miss Eleanor was a grown-up lady, for goodness' sakes, and I wouldn't have thought she would act so silly, but she did.

And Papa didn't mind at all!

We stood there until my legs started to go numb while Miss Eleanor asked questions about Papa and his "adventures in mining."

"Charming young woman," said Papa as we went up the steps after she left. He acted all plumped up like a rooster, not remembering at all, I guess, what he'd said in Sacramento about Miss Eleanor not knowing how to dress.

"Mr. Edwards!" Charlie said, opening the door and grinning all over. "You going to find big silver mine?"

"Could be, Charlie," said Papa.

Charlie acted really pleased to see Papa. Mrs. MacKay didn't. She came down the stairs toward us, her eyes snapping as though she'd swallowed fire-crackers.

Charlie slid away toward the kitchen. I wished I could slink away too, but I don't think Mrs. MacKay even saw me.

"So, John," she said, "you're back."

"Like the bad penny," said Papa.

"Where have you been?"

"Tonopah, my darling girl," Papa said, and then he kissed her very *unsanitarily*, if you ask me, which nobody does, of course. "I've been off to make our fortune."

"Without informing me?"

He didn't answer her but turned to me and said, "Where's the rest of the family, Abby?"

"Looking for work, Papa."

"Ah, the diligent ants. They take after your most admirable Uncle George, no doubt. . . ."

Papa's mouth twisted quite oddly.

"Fortunately for the world," Mrs. MacKay said, "we aren't all grasshoppers."

They were talking about that story where the ants worked all summer laying up supplies for bad weather. The grasshopper made nasty remarks about the hard-working ants while he led a merry old life all summer and almost froze to death come winter. I didn't think Papa much liked being called a grasshopper.

"We had a shutdown while you were chasing gold," Mrs. MacKay said.

"Silver . . . it could be a new bonanza!"

"You left the mill in charge of Jesse Smith!"

"Jesse could handle it."

"Jesse did handle it."

"He's a good man. Knows the mill better than I do."

"I expect my orders to be followed, John."

"Orders?" said Papa.

The electricity crackled between them. I looked from one to the other. Aunt Eunice always said Papa couldn't abide taking orders. He hadn't worked for anybody but himself much, except when he worked for the government survey.

"And you sent me these children . . . these very large children. . . ."

"I knew you could handle them."

He swung her around and kissed her again. I guess that was the right thing to do, as her mad began to sort of leak away and pretty soon they got all lovey-dovey. It was rather disgusting for people their age.

"Well," said Mrs. MacKay finally, "I have missed you."

"I knew it," said Papa. "So when are we going to tie the knot?"

"There are still a few details to work out, John."

"You don't need female fripperies to make you beautiful. You're gorgeous enough already!"

"How you do go on!" She laughed and sounded pleased, but still said something about Papa going to see her lawyer. He said he would. He didn't, not right away, because Damaris and Joel came in, anxious to tell about their new jobs, Damaris with Dr. Merrick and Joel at the power company.

Papa said he was proud of their "get-up-and-go" but that they could quit as soon as he made his big strike. Then we would build a house up on Nob Hill. He and Joel would wear carnations in their button-holes and smoke two-dollar cigars, and Mrs. MacKay and Damaris and I would drip with diamonds and pearls and have imported lace on our chemises and bloomers.

I'm certain positive Aunt Eunice wouldn't approve of Papa talking about our underwear, and Mrs. MacKay didn't say much. I've seen her things hanging on the line after the wash boy comes. Mrs. MacKay already has lace on her bloomers.

Papa had a room in Oakland near the mill, but when he came back, he slept in Mrs. MacKay's library to be near us.

"Until the wedding," he said with a wink.

The lovey-dovey sweet-talking lasted two whole days until the morning Mrs. MacKay asked Papa if he had picked up the papers from her lawyer.

It was a really nice morning. The wind had blown away the fog early, and Papa said Mrs. MacKay should

play hooky and have lunch with him out at a restaurant called the Cliff House.

Mrs. MacKay shook her head and said she didn't
have time to fritter away. That's when she asked if
he had seen the lawyer.

He hadn't.

Mrs. MacKay said he was about as dependable as
a flea.

Papa said he reckoned he wasn't cut out to be a
ladies' lackey, stuck on his hat, and marched out the
door.

"Your father is undependable," Mrs. MacKay said
as it slammed behind him.

We knew that.

We could depend more on Uncle George than on
Papa.

We could depend more on the Maharajah of Mar-
rakesh (if there is such a person) than on Papa.

Damaris and Joel and Mrs. MacKay went off to
work. Papa just went off . . . without saying *where* he
was going.

I sat down to eat my breakfast alone, and thought
about calling Mrs. Benton about a job. I didn't know
if I should with Papa back, but it got lonesome in that
house with nothing to do.

Ah Sing banged his pots and cleavers in the kitchen,
and Charlie was busy with his pots of turpentine and
wax. Papa came in and slung a packet of papers on

the table, which I guessed were the lawyer ones Mrs. MacKay wanted, because he said he'd signed his life away and hoped she was satisfied.

"All the diligent ants have gone, eh? Well, then," he said, "it's up to us grasshoppers to enjoy life."

I didn't much like being called a grasshopper either and was going to say so, when he said, "Well, Abby, since I have a table reserved for lunch and Mistress Molly has gone off in a snit, how about putting on your best bonnet and keeping me company?"

I wished he'd asked me first, not just because Mrs. MacKay was mad at him, and I didn't have a best bonnet, but I put on my old sailor hat and went along anyway.

We took a trolley and then the steam car way out along the cliffs past Land's End to the Cliff House. It looked like a decoration for a wedding cake. The ocean was blue as ink, and it was all so extremely beautiful that I was secretly glad he and Mrs. MacKay had had what I expect Aunt Eunice would call a lovers' quarrel.

I surely wouldn't say that myself, as I don't think it is proper for a papa to be a lover. I would call it a plain old fight.

We sat by a window, watched the ocean, and had a Perfectly Elegant lunch.

We'd finished our chicken in *wine* sauce. Another thing not to write to Aunt Eunice. She was once president of the Estes Temperance Society and would be *scandalized!*

Then the waiter brought in the dessert and set it on the table, took a match, and lit it!

I dropped my napkin, leaped out of my chair, and knocked over my water glass.

"Papa! It's on fire!" I said.

"Crème brûlée," he said quite calmly.

It wasn't an accident or a terrible mistake.

They dump *brandy* (which is *alcohol*) all over a sort of custard and set it on fire. On purpose.

"Well," I said as the waiter mopped up the water, "we never set fire to desserts back home, not on purpose." Mrs. Smith Kenyon burned them sometimes, but then it was a mistake.

In spite of feeling foolish over the *crème brûlée* and spilling my water, which was very embarrassing, I would have had a good time if Papa hadn't looked so gloomy. When I asked him what was wrong, he just said that he'd better get on over to the mill or Mrs. MacKay would start hunting his scalp.

He stayed glum almost all the way back to Mrs. MacKay's until who should we see waiting at the corner for our car but Miss Eleanor and the Colonel. The wind was giving Miss Eleanor trouble with her hat again. As they climbed aboard the trolley, she held it down with one hand and her skirts down with the other.

"Abby!" she said. "I called on you this morning to ask . . . to tell you I saw Mrs. Benton again, and she is really most anxious to talk to you and your father."

She introduced Papa and the Colonel, and my goodness, you would have thought they had known each other all their lives instead of just having met that instant.

Miss Eleanor looked happy. She whispered to me that she was doing the desserts for Mrs. Wheeler. She was doing the soups and salads too. Mrs. Wheeler did well enough on the chops and roasts. The other boarders seemed very happy with the improved cooking. Miss Eleanor was paying for their board and room and had a little left over for lessons.

"Lessons? What are you studying?" I asked.

"The dance. That's what I wanted to tell you. Mrs. Wheeler is encouraging me, but Daddy thinks I've taken leave of my senses."

"What kind of dance?" I asked.

"Modern dance," said Miss Eleanor, but she didn't seem to be paying much attention to me. She was looking at Papa.

"Perhaps you could take lessons too, Abby. Your daddy seems a broad-minded man. I'm sure he wouldn't object if you took up the dance."

"No, I expect he wouldn't." He might not even notice, I thought. I had the feeling that all three of us were sort of the side dish in Papa's life, not the main course.

"Daddy says all we do at Miss Vivian's studio is sashay around in nightgowns, but that isn't so. Our costumes are very artistic and graceful. Self-expression is so fulfilling. Don't you think, Abby?"

"I guess so," I said, trying to picture Miss Eleanor trailing around in her nightie.

Papa and the Colonel talked about mining, how the latest strike was copper. And how much money was to be made for those who got in on the ground floor, though Papa said silver was still king.

The Colonel said he would be mighty interested in taking a flyer if only he had not lost his money in the Crash of '95.

He glared at Miss Eleanor as though it had been her fault. Then he noticed where we were and said they'd gone past their stop.

Papa tipped his hat as they got off the trolley.

"Nice young woman," he said. "Not full of spit and vinegar. Like some."

Then he frowned, and I wondered if he had Mrs. MacKay in mind.

NINETEEN

It was Wednesday.

I'd been dreaming of Mama and felt so lonesome for her I could have bawled. Instead I blew my nose, crawled out of bed, and got dressed. Damaris was all ready for work. She pinned her hat on and asked if I was sick again. I wasn't. Lonesome doesn't count as sick.

Damaris and Joel had to leave early. Papa and Mrs. MacKay were going to leave early too, so once again I settled down for breakfast by myself. It's not much fun to eat alone.

I looked out at the eucalyptus in the garden wet from the fog, and wished I were back home with Uncle George and Aunt Eunice and Dolly Raymond. I would even have been glad to see Mary Margaret Vincent!

Mrs. MacKay came in buttoning her gloves. She took a look at me, and then *she* asked if I felt all right.

"Yes, ma'am," I said.

"Feeling homesick?"

"I guess so."

She was quiet a minute. Then she said, "It's a bad feeling . . . as if you have no place in the world where you belong. As though even God doesn't know where to find you . . . but He does."

I looked at her most astonished! Damaris had made sure Joel and I went to church Sunday, but Mrs. MacKay hadn't gone, not that I knew of, so it was a surprise to have her talk as though . . . as though she was acquainted with God *personally*.

"Pretty soon you'll feel at home here, Abby," she said.

I thought that was very nice of her. Mrs. MacKay was not so bad after all.

Not that I wanted her for a stepmother. Not that I wanted *anyone* for a stepmother, trying to take Mama's place, which of course no one could. Not ever! Not in a million trillion years!

Papa was working in the library. Mrs. MacKay wanted him to leave with her, but he said he had to stay and talk to "a money man."

"I thought Sam Stritch was financing this mining enterprise," she said.

"Sam's in, but he doesn't have enough capital for a first-class operation. Now, if I could just persuade you, Molly. . . ."

"You can't. I learned about poverty young, John. It's made me cautious. About mines. And money. And other things."

"Not too cautious, I trust," Papa said.

I think he must have kissed her then because she laughed and said, "Not too cautious."

"Come home early," he said. "We'll make plans."

"I will," she promised.

Charlie brought me my eggs, and after Mrs. MacKay left, he went into the library and started talking to Papa about Tonopah. Charlie wanted to go too, to make his fortune. The way Charlie (and Ah Sing) gambled, even if they made a fortune, they'd probably lose it at fan-tan, but Papa said he'd keep him in mind when he got the grubstake together. *If* he got it together.

"Missee not help?" Charlie said.

"Afraid not," said Papa.

I was finishing up my eggs when Papa came in and asked me if I wanted to go for a walk. He had a couple of hours before his appointment with the money man. The wind was blowing away the fog, and he said it would blow the cobwebs out of our brains too.

As we walked downhill toward the Bay, I asked, "Are there fan-tan games in Tonopah?"

"There's all kinds of gambling going on in Tonopah," Papa said. "Mining's a gamble. But you can't even get in the game without a stake."

It made me feel very grown-up to have Papa talk about business to me. Of course, I was the only one around at the time for him to talk to.

Papa started asking about Aunt Eunice and Uncle George. I wondered if he wanted them to help with the grubstake. I knew Uncle George couldn't, even if Aunt Eunice would let him, which was extremely unlikely.

I told about their losing the hardware store. Then I guess I did go on a bit how Uncle George had patched up our roof when it leaked, taught Joel how to fix the steps and the pump, and helped us when Mama was so sick.

Papa was quiet for a minute. Then he said, "Think a lot of old George, don't you?"

I nodded and wondered if I'd talked too much about Uncle George.

Down at the Embarcadero we saw a most horrible sight.

A man came down to the edge of the water with a sack of kittens and threw them in!

The poor skinny mother cat followed along meowing most piteously. She went straight into the water after the sack and came back carrying one poor half-drowned kitten. She licked it and licked it, until it gave one little meow.

"The mother instinct," said Papa, "is quite remarkable. I may not have been much of a father, but I did see that you had a good mother, Abby."

"Yes, Papa," I said.

I started to snuffle away, thinking about Mama, and, of course, I couldn't find my handkerchief because I'd forgotten to bring one.

Papa reached into his pocket and handed me his.

And then I thought, What if Papa hadn't pulled me out of the lake when I was little? Why, I could have been drowned just like the rest of those kittens. I shivered and snuffled some more, and Papa said he thought some hot tea was in order and he knew just the place to get it.

"What about the grubstake?" I asked.

"A couple of cream puffs aren't going to make that much difference," he said.

We had more than tea and a cream puff.

Papa took me to a shop where we ordered little pastry horns filled with cream and miniature chocolate éclairs. Papa said I would probably end up with the stomachache, but I said if I did, it was worth it.

Out on the street after we finished our tea we ran into Miss Eleanor again. She was carrying a shopping bag with a bit of something white and filmy showing.

"My costume," she said, tucking it back in. "For my lesson, you know."

"Lesson?" I said. "Oh, yes, in the dance. Are you on your way downtown for your lesson?"

She nodded, and Papa said he was on his way downtown too, so he would go along with Miss Eleanor if she didn't mind. She got all pink and said she wouldn't mind in the least. She would be quite delighted to hear about all his Adventures, as she would have dearly loved to be born a man and go on Adventures herself.

Papa said it was sometimes an uncomfortable life, but Miss Eleanor said she didn't think a person should mind a little discomfort as long as there was Adventure.

Papa sent me on home, and the last I saw of them they were climbing on the streetcar, with Miss Eleanor still talking about Adventure.

I guess everything would have been all right if Mrs. MacKay hadn't been downtown and seen Papa get off the streetcar with Miss Eleanor.

That night she and Papa had one great big old fight. As soon as he got one foot in the door, Mrs. MacKay started in.

"Who," she said, "was that great tall bean pole I saw you talking to in the middle of Market Street this afternoon?" The minute she said bean pole I knew she meant Miss Eleanor.

From there I don't know exactly how they got to money and the grubstake, but Papa said, "Where's your spirit of adventure?"

Mrs. MacKay said she had her fill of dodging rattlesnakes and scorpions and picking grit from her coffee with Mr. Travers (that was her first husband) and she didn't intend to do it again. Papa said she didn't trust him with her welfare.

And she said, "With my welfare possibly. Not with my money!"

Papa said, "If that's the way you feel, I'll leave."

"While you're at it, why don't you go see if that giraffe will give you money to sink down some useless mine shaft!"

"Pack," said Papa to us. "We're not welcome here."

"The kids don't have to go," Mrs. MacKay said. "I wouldn't turn them out."

"Pack," said Papa.

And we did.

Damaris and I didn't say one word as we trudged upstairs. I'd just begun to like Mrs. MacKay. And besides, she had the nicest house I'd ever lived in, and I wondered dismally if we would ever have a real place to call home.

I stuffed everything on top of my Idea Book and snapped my valise shut. Damaris folded her things neatly just so, and that took longer, but we finally finished and went downstairs to where Joel and Papa were waiting. Papa seemed to have recovered his good spirits.

"Well," he said cheerfully, "if Her Majesty won't come with me to Tonopah and make a fortune, I bet I know three people who will!"

Three? Us?

I had a mixed-up feeling inside. Wasn't that what we'd wanted? What I'd wanted anyway. Papa all to our own selves. So why did I feel so peculiar, with my heart thumping around in my chest like a drum?

"We'll be a real family," Papa said. "One for all and all for one. Who said that?"

"The Three Musketeers," said Joel, looking at Damaris, who didn't say anything, but bit her lip until I thought it would bleed.

We didn't go to Tonopah that evening.

Instead we took the trolley to Mrs. Wheeler's boardinghouse.

TWENTY

Mrs. Wheeler greeted Papa as though he were her long-lost child, and he gave her a great smacking kiss.

"Dear boy! What a delight to see you," she said, and immediately offered him dinner. When he said "No, thanks" to dinner, she said he should at least have some tea and molasses cookies.

Papa said thanks, but he didn't believe he cared for any cookies. I thought he probably knew Mrs. Wheeler wasn't much of a cook.

"They're fresh-baked," she said.

"No, thanks, Melisande." (Imagine an old lady like Mrs. Wheeler having a name like Melisande! It sounds like something out of an opera.)

"How old are your youngsters, John?" she asked. Papa couldn't remember our ages, not even mine, and I will be thirteen on the Fourth of July, which doesn't seem hard to remember, but Papa had to ask.

Joel helped himself to a cookie. Mrs. Wheeler kept holding out the plate, so I took one to be polite and bit into it cautiously. It was very good!

"Your Miss Eleanor made them," said Mrs. Wheeler. "I can't thank you enough for sending that girl to me. But what can I do for you, John?"

"I need a favor, Melisande."

"Did Molly chuck you out?"

"We had a difference of opinion."

"Need beds?"

"For a night or two. Tomorrow or the next day we'll have to see to outfitting these youngsters and buying our tickets, and then we'll be on our way to Nevada."

Outfitting? Did he mean new clothes? From what Mrs. MacKay said, I shouldn't have thought we needed new ones.

"How I envy you!" Mrs. Wheeler sniffed. She sniffs a lot. When she does, her nose with the wart twitches. "And Molly's not going with you?"

"No," said Papa.

"She'll be sorry. Come on, kiddies, I'll show you where to bunk."

Mrs. Wheeler led us up three flights of stairs to the attic, talking all the time about how she and the Mister (that was her husband before he died) and Papa had all been together mining in Colorado, in the Good Old Days.

"Joel," Damaris whispered, "we have to talk," and he nodded.

"Sorry to put you youngsters up here," Mrs. Wheeler said as she huffed to a stop at the top of the stairs.

"We're sorry to trouble you," Damaris said.

"No trouble, dearie," she said. "You'll have to use the kerosene lamp, though. No gas laid on up here, or electricity. Guess that's the latest folderol the boarders will be wanting."

"About electricity . . ." Joel opened his mouth probably planning to explain everything he knew about electricity (which was a lot) and all he was about to learn working at the power plant (which was more). Damaris squelched him with a look. After Mrs. Wheeler left, he knocked on our door.

"What's up, sis?" he asked.

"It's about Papa, Joel," Damaris said.

"What about him?"

"I don't intend to go with him now that I'm working for Dr. Merrick."

"But he expects you to!" I said. "Joel . . . you tell her she has to come!"

Joel shook his head. "It's not right for us to quit our jobs right after we've been hired on, Abby."

"You aren't going either? But Papa is counting on you both!"

"I know," Damaris said. "I'm sorry, but . . . we have to think what's best for us, because Papa . . . Papa does what he wants to do. . . ."

"He doesn't always think what's best for us," Joel said.

Nobody said anything for a minute. I was thinking

about Damaris, how she always thought Papa was Positively Perfect. Now it seemed as though she had changed her mind.

"What about the sprout here?" said Joel, pointing to me.

Sprout, indeed! Talking about me as though I were . . . a *vegetable*!

"We can take care of her between us," Damaris said.

"I can take care of my own self!" I said. "Besides, I'm going with Papa! And when I come back with my pockets full of silver, well, I'll treat you all to dinner out at . . . at the Cliff House!"

"You don't just pick up silver off the ground that easy, sprout!"

Both he and Damaris tried to talk me out of it. Joel kept reminding me of stuff I'd rather he didn't—scorpions and rattlesnakes and such—but I just closed my ears and wouldn't listen.

"I don't care! I'm going with Papa!"

"We'll talk about it in the morning," Damaris said, and we all went to bed, but I don't think any of us went right to sleep.

I thought about going with Papa by myself, and how I would take care of him and cook for him. Well, I wasn't a really good cook yet, but I could make pretty good pancakes.

I went to sleep thinking about pancakes and woke

up real early dreaming about a spider the size of a dinner plate and a snake with lemon-colored eyes and a forked tongue. I scared myself so I couldn't get back to sleep and started wondering if maybe I should chicken out of going with Papa. Or if he'd let me.

It was just getting light when I got dressed and went downstairs. Miss Eleanor was in the kitchen already up to her elbows in dough.

"Abby!" she said. "What a surprise!"

When I explained about Papa and me and how I was (probably) going to help him hunt for silver, she said, "How exciting!" and her eyes got all starry.

"Do you think so?" I said.

"Of course! What an Adventure! I do so envy you!"

For breakfast Miss Eleanor baked biscuits and an apple-and-walnut coffee cake. Her biscuits drenched in butter and strawberry jam just melted in our mouths.

Papa finished his third piece of coffee cake, leaned back, and said, "That was excellent, Melisande!"

"Miss Eleanor's doing," Mrs. Wheeler said. "The girl's a jewel."

"Pretty too," said Papa.

Mrs. Wheeler didn't treat Miss Eleanor like a cook, not like Mrs. MacKay did Ah Sing with his cleaver. He ate in the kitchen, but Miss Eleanor took her apron off and came in to eat with the rest of us.

"My compliments to the cook," Papa said as she slipped into her chair.

I have decided Papa looks at most ladies in an interested way, even old ones like Mrs. Wheeler, and they usually get all fussed when he does. Miss Eleanor certainly did. She turned pink and said it was nothing and my, isn't it warm in here, which it wasn't really, as Mrs. Wheeler is pretty stingy with coal for the stoves.

Joel ate until his eyeballs bulged, and I ate quite a lot myself. I helped myself to a cup of coffee, which made me feel quite grown-up. I don't think Damaris noticed or she would have said I was too young.

Joel grinned at me and said, "You'll stunt your growth, Abby."

I don't know whether that's true or not. I didn't want to take a chance, though, so I put in lots of milk just in case. My coffee turned out mostly coffee-flavored milk.

The Colonel and Papa were talking away at a great rate about mining.

"Papa . . ." Damaris tried to interrupt.

"Later, princess," he said.

"You still working on the money angle, John?" Mrs. Wheeler asked. "I'd sure admire to help you if I could."

"Likewise," said the Colonel. "Unfortunately I find myself in straitened circumstances."

He glared at Miss Eleanor, who got up from the table saying she must get more biscuits. I think she just wanted to get away from the Colonel, as we were all already "stuffed like Christmas geese," as Papa said.

"All Eleanor needs to do to put us on easy street is to marry Quentin Jerome," the Colonel complained.

"Jerome?" said Mrs. Wheeler. "Don't blame her for turning him down. Dull as dirty socks and mean as a toad to his kids. A blooming fortune hunter, to boot!"

"No fortune to hunt if the girl doesn't marry."

"Any reason it has to be to Jerome?"

"No, but Eleanor's mighty backward with beaus."

There was a big clatter and smash as Miss Eleanor came through the swinging door from the kitchen and dropped the plate of biscuits. Papa and I went to help pick up the pieces.

"Thank you," Miss Eleanor said, still bent over. Her eyes looked funny. Funny peculiar.

"You're welcome," said Papa.

"Papa . . ." Damaris interrupted.

I knew she was still trying to tell him about not wanting to go hunting for silver, but Papa wouldn't let her. He pulled out his pocket watch and said, "It'll have to wait, princess, but this afternoon we'll go see to your new outfits. Can't have our prospectors in petticoats!"

After everybody left and I was helping Miss Eleanor clear off the table, she asked, "How much money does your daddy need, Abby?"

"Lots," I said. "I don't know exactly how much."

"And this Mrs. MacKay he is going to marry . . ."

"*Was* going to marry. She says she won't pour her good money down any old empty mine hole."

"I see," said Miss Eleanor, looking thoughtful.

I couldn't figure out exactly what she thought she saw, and she didn't say.

TWENTY-ONE

It kept getting closer and closer to the Fourth of July and my birthday. We were still at Mrs. Wheeler's; in spite of what Papa had said when we came, it seemed he was still trying to get the grubstake together.

Finally, it really was the Fourth. I woke up to the sound of firecrackers crackling way off in Chinatown. It reminded me of last year back in Estes with Mama, and I thought it was just going to be a lonesome old Purely Awful day.

It was cold and foggy and Papa had gone off without saying one word, so I knew he had forgotten again. I made up my mind I would just pretend I wasn't disappointed so nobody would know. It's worse to be disappointed and have everybody in the world feel sorry for you.

Then when I went downstairs, I saw Damaris and Joel hiding packages in the dining room, so I knew at least *they* hadn't forgotten.

Joel had to start teasing again. He does tease something fierce about how close I'd come to being named Independence Day Edwards on account of being born on the Fourth of July.

He said, "We could have called you Indie for short. Or Dence . . . for Dense!" And then he laughed like a perfect fiend. Honestly! Joel can be a great trial!

After noon the sun came out, and the day didn't turn out Purely Awful after all.

Papa came back in time for the parade. The downtown stores were all draped with bunting, and the drum and bugle corps and the fire brigades looked perfectly splendid in their uniforms. The Colonel and Mrs. Wheeler went with us. Miss Eleanor didn't, and I wondered why.

When we got back, I found out.

The table was decorated with red and white streamers, and she had baked a perfectly elegant cake with stars and flags and my name on top in red, white, and blue icing!

Joel said, "Happy thirteenth, squirt," and gave me a little mechanical merry-go-round that played "Clementine"; Damaris had bought me a nice, fat, unwritten-in new Idea Book.

Miss Eleanor gave me a hair ribbon, and the Colonel a framed copy of the Declaration of Independence, which I don't quite know what to do with, but I thanked him anyway. Mrs. Wheeler gave me one of those paperweights you shake and it looks like it's snowing.

And Papa didn't forget! Or if he did, somebody reminded him. He handed me a small box. In it was a thin silver chain and a pendant set with bits of blue rock that Papa called turquoise.

"My! How lovely!" said Miss Eleanor.

"Yes," said Papa, looking at Miss Eleanor with that little quirky smile. Then he gave me another present. A compass.

"So we don't lose our youngest prospector," he said.

"Thank you, Papa," I said, dearly hoping I wouldn't ever get lost and have to use it, because I didn't know how, though Papa said I could learn.

Joel looked at Damaris, and she gave a little nod.

"Papa," she said, "we must talk to you."

Here it comes, I thought, at last!

"Well, all right, princess. What is it?"

She took a deep breath and said, "I'm not going to Nevada with you, Papa."

"Not going!"

"I'm going to stay here at Mrs. Wheeler's, if that's all right with her, and work for Dr. Viola. Dr. Viola Merrick."

"That woman doctor?" Papa made it sound like a disease, and I saw Damaris's cheeks get red.

"Papa, really. . . . Dr. Merrick is a fine physician!"

Papa fussed a bit but finally said he guessed she was old enough to make up her mind and that the rest of us would just have to get along without her.

"Right, Joel?" said Papa.

Joel cleared his throat and said, seeing as how he'd just gotten on at the power company, he didn't believe he should go either.

Poor Papa, I thought. When he finally wanted to take us with him, nobody wanted to go except me, and I only partly wanted to go.

I partly wanted to when I thought about keeping house for Papa and having him all to myself. And partly I didn't. Especially when Joel kept reminding me about scorpions and rattlesnakes and such and telling me I'd have to take a bath in a bucket, as there wouldn't be much water in the desert, though I told myself he was just teasing.

"Electricity is the coming thing, Papa," Joel was saying.

Papa said he was some disappointed but that Joel didn't need to explain the advantages of a bright young fellow getting in on the ground floor of the electrical business.

"What about school?" asked Miss Eleanor.

"I've graduated from eighth grade," Joel said. "That's as far as most fellows go, but I plan to go on part-time."

"Well, Abby," Papa said, "I guess it's up to you and me to make the family fortune."

"Yes, Papa," I said, hesitating only the tiniest bit of a second.

"Did you get your grubstake together, John?" Mrs. Wheeler asked.

"Enough to start."

"Molly MacKay hasn't changed her mind about helping out?"

"No," said Papa.

Then he looked at Miss Eleanor and smiled.

"Miss Eleanor," he said, "you have flour on your nose."

She turned red and rubbed it off, and Papa said, "It was really quite fetching."

The next day right after breakfast he trotted me down to a hole-in-the-wall store that sold boots and buggy whips and shovels and axes and I don't know what all else, and I found out what Papa meant by a new outfit.

He bought me boy's boots, a big felt hat, overalls that had to be hiked up practically to my armpits, a couple of shirts and a canteen for water and a bandanna he said would come in handy to wipe off sweat in the desert.

He also bought me a sharp knife. He said if a rattlesnake bit me, I was to slash an **X** between the fang marks and suck out the blood so I wouldn't die. He didn't say what I was to do if I sat on one.

"Guess that's it," said Papa, reaching into his pocket for a gold piece to pay for it all. "If we forgot anything, we'll get it in Tonopah along with the burros."

"What's a burro?" I asked.

"A donkey. Useful animal in rough country."

He had the lot sent out to Mrs. Wheeler's and then

bought sandwiches in an Italian delicatessen that smelled of garlic and had long strings of salami hanging from the ceiling. We ate our sandwiches down at the Embarcadero while we watched the fishing boats bob about out on the Bay. The water chuckled up and slapped the rocks and pier.

"You fell in the lake when you were a little squirt, Abby," Papa said. "Popped right up like a cork."

"And you hauled me out by the hair."

"Lucky I did."

"Lucky?"

"Saved the pick of the litter. . . ."

That made me sort of sigh inside. Damaris was the princess, but I was "chicken" or "sprout" or "the pick of the litter"!

"The only one"—Papa clapped me on the shoulder—"to stick by her dad."

He whistled a tune as we turned up Market Street, and I followed along.

How come when you get what you want, it turns out not quite the way you thought? I'd wanted to find Papa, wanted him to take an interest in me. And we were going out together to hunt silver, and I felt excited. But why did I feel scared and sick to my stomach too?

Just then someone called, "Yoo-hoo, Mr. Edwards!"

Mrs. Benton came sailing out of a ladies' corset-and-glove shop, a parcel under her arm and Buster dragging along behind.

"Babby!" Buster hurled himself at me. When I picked him up, he planted a wet kiss on my cheek and then wriggled back down to the ground.

"Mr. Edwards!" Mrs. Benton said, keeping a firm hold on Buster's leash. "I have been leaving messages for you at Mrs. MacKay's."

"Yes?" said Papa.

"Just a minute, darling," she said to Buster, who was tugging at her parcel. "You want to hold Mama's package for her? Do be careful of it. That's a little love. . . ."

"I would like very much to employ Abigail. She was so good with the children on the train, especially Buster." She looked down at Buster happily chewing on the corner of her parcel.

Papa said he was sorry but I was going with him to Nevada.

"Nevada!"

Mrs. Benton told Papa she was "horrified" to find him proposing to take "this child" (me) off into the woolly wilds, tramping about in the sun, ruining my complexion, getting blisters on my feet. . . .

"No blisters on her feet," said Papa with a twinkle in his eye. "We'll get her a burro to ride." Besides which he said it would be fall before we started any real prospecting.

Mrs. Benton said what could he be thinking of, and what would happen to my education, and that I wouldn't be fit for decent society.

"Madam," said Papa, "just what would you have me do with her?"

"Send her with me. To the Islands. It would be a wonderful opportunity for Abby. We would see that she went to school. And she would be a great help with Buster. He's such an active child. . . ."

We looked down at Buster.

"My land!" said Mrs. Benton.

"Hat," said Buster, grinning happily.

Mrs. Benton's brand-new pink corset was perched on Buster's head. The laces dangled around his ears.

Some choice, I thought.

A burro or Buster.

TWENTY-TWO

Papa plucked Mrs. Benton's corset off Buster's head and rewrapped it as though stuffing ladies' corsets into sacks was a most ordinary circumstance.

"The Islands have magnificent scenery," said Papa, going on about palm trees and trade winds and such.

"You've been there?" Mrs. Benton asked as Papa handed back her parcel.

"Indeed," said Papa.

Then he started talking about the Islands' splendid specimens of humanity (and *womanity*, though I believe Papa made up that word) who were free, he said, "to gambol as true children of nature in the emerald seas, unrestricted by the constraints and constrictions of civilized accoutrements." (I think he was talking about corsets.)

"Indeed," said Mrs. Benton.

Mrs. Benton's "indeed" had an altogether different sound to it than Papa's. I don't think she liked his talking about "womanity" and grass skirts and such.

"Please think it over, Mr. Edwards," she said.

"You want to think it over, Abby?" Papa said.

I swallowed hard, thinking about the palm trees and emerald seas. Then I looked at Buster twirling away at the end of his harness and shook my head.

"I knew I could count on you, partner," Papa said.

"Yes, Papa," I said.

If Papa wanted me to go with him, I had to go. Especially since Joel and Damaris wouldn't, and Mrs. MacKay wouldn't either. I just couldn't let him think nobody wanted to go with him.

I think maybe Mrs. MacKay wanted to make up with Papa when she came by Mrs. Wheeler's the next day. She and Papa and the delivery boy with my outfit all met on the front stoop. For a minute she and Papa just looked at each other.

Then she said, "Did you buy out a store, John?"

"It's my prospecting outfit," I said.

"So you are all going."

"Just me," I said.

"She'd cut off her nose for you," she said. (Which is Distinctly Untrue!)

"Abby has a heart," Papa said, "not an adding machine where her heart ought to be. Did you have some reason for this visit, Mrs. MacKay?"

"I brought your letters. You haven't bothered to pick them up."

Then she said, "Abby, if you get tired of grit and heat, you can come live with me."

"I'm sure Abby thanks you," said Papa, "but she'll be staying with me."

"Have you thought to give her a choice? You ought to! You could take Charlie instead. He's mad to go."

Mrs. MacKay gave Papa a glittering sort of a glance, handed over the letters, and left. Mrs. Wheeler poked her head out from the kitchen and said, "Did she change her mind about going?"

"No," said Papa, handing me my letters.

There was one from Aunt Eunice, one from Dolly Raymond, and one (I almost fell over in surprise) from Mary Margaret Vincent!

Aunt Eunice said Uncle George still hadn't found work in Illinois and they were thinking of moving again.

Dolly is my best friend in the world, but her letter sounded as though nothing at all had happened in Estes since we left. Mary Margaret told me more. She said Mr. Buttchenbacher and his new wife were expecting a baby, and Mrs. Smith Kenyon already had one (her seventh). And then right down at the bottom of the page she wrote, "Pa is thinking of moving to California too, so we may be seeing you soon!"

Thank goodness I'm going with Papa! I thought, which wasn't very nice of me, I guess.

Everybody had to put in their two cents about my new clothes.

Miss Eleanor thought they were "terribly exciting."

Damaris said the more she thought about it, the

surer she was Mama wouldn't want me traipsing about the desert.

"Your mother didn't mind 'traipsing about' herself," Papa said, "before she had you children."

Joel said, "If you strike it rich, Abby, you can forget about that dinner at the Cliff House you promised. Just build me a laboratory like Mr. Thomas Alva Edison's. . . ."

"She shouldn't go at all!" Damaris said.

"Mrs. MacKay says I should be the one to choose," I said.

"What?" boomed the Colonel. "Let a female choose? Tell 'em what's what, my boy. That's the ticket!"

The Colonel is certainly a big blowhard windbag, and I would have liked to stick a pin in him and watch him collapse like a stuck balloon!

When I get told what to do, especially in that bossy tone of voice, and even if it was what I wanted to do in the first place, it always makes me want to do exactly the opposite!

Papa said it would be a Splendid Adventure, that we would go up into the mountains, and camp with the sky for our roof and the ground for our pillow, which sounded beautiful, but not awfully comfortable.

"You mean you aren't even going to be in town?" Damaris said.

"Can't prospect in town, girl!" said Mrs. Wheeler,

and I began to wish I hadn't been so quick to say I'd go.

"What about when school starts, Papa?" Damaris's chin stuck out with that stubborn tilt to it.

"School, pooh!" said Mrs. Wheeler, the wart on her nose trembling. "What counts is the school of experience! Why, the Mister and me, we neither one of us went past the third grade and we did all right, leastways we did until the Mister up and died."

"Abby should go to school," Damaris said. "Please, leave her with me, Papa, or let her go with the Bentons."

"I'm going with Papa!" I said.

"Bully for you!" said Mrs. Wheeler.

After breakfast the next day I told Papa I was all packed, and Mrs. Wheeler said I could leave my regular clothes with her and if he was ready to go, I could jump right into my overalls and boots. I wanted to get going before I had too much time to think about sand and snakes and sleeping on the ground with wiggly crawlies.

"I've been thinking . . ." he said.

"You've been listening to Damaris!"

"She makes sense," he said.

"Don't you want me to come, Papa?"

"It's not that. I'm trying to think what's best for you, for once. I'm afraid I haven't been too good at that in the past, princess."

He called me *princess*. He'd always called Damaris

princess, not me, but my mind was so busy scurrying about I only half noticed.

"Abby, I know you said you'd go with me, but what about Mrs. Benton's offer? Be honest now."

I was Positively Torn.

It was the first time Papa ever wanted me to go with him. I would have him all to myself. And I couldn't let Papa think *nobody* wanted to go with him. On the other hand, beaches and palm trees (even with Buster thrown in) sounded awfully nice.

"I'd like to do both," I said finally.

"You can't do both."

"I'd like to go to the Islands except . . ."

"Except what?"

"I don't want you to be lonesome."

"Thanks, princess." He smiled at me. Then he said, "It's not right to leave the decision up to you."

Then he just sat there, not saying *anything*!

"Well?" I said. "What is it?"

"What's what?" he said with the same kind of teasing grin Joel has.

"Papa! What's the decision?"

"You'll go with the Bentons . . ."

"No!"

". . . and acquire 'culture and social know-how,' as Mrs. Benton says. But, young lady"—he shook a finger in my face like a schoolmaster—"I expect you to come back knowing how to make flower leis and do the hula dance."

"Oh, Papa. . . ."

He patted me on the shoulder, and I reached up on tiptoes and kissed him.

"Friends?" he said.

"Friends," I said, and he squeezed my hand.

"That's my girl," he said.

"But you'll be alone, Papa," I objected.

"It won't be the first time," he said.

TWENTY-THREE

I needn't have worried about Papa.

He didn't go alone.

Sometimes I feel like my life is written on the sand, and every so often a big wind swoops down and blows it in eleventeen million different directions!

After Papa said I was to go to the Islands with the Bentons, I went to help them pack.

Buster, of course, managed to fall into an open trunk, and the lid snapped shut. Fortunately I heard him kicking and hollering. When I hauled him out, he was wiping his nose on Mrs. Benton's brand-new embroidered bloomers.

He was red in the face from screaming bloody murder, but otherwise whole and unhurt. I told Mrs. Benton we'd best take a couple of extra harnesses on board ship, and she agreed that might be a good idea.

All the while I kept thinking about Papa going to Tonopah alone.

Like I say, I needn't have worried.

Papa didn't go alone. He didn't go with Mrs. MacKay either.

He went with Charlie, Mrs. MacKay's houseboy. Charlie was wearing overalls and a cowboy hat and had a pack practically as big as he was strapped to his back. It was topped off with a black iron skillet Joel said was liable to fall off and brain him if he wasn't careful.

Colonel Spencer went too.

So did Miss Eleanor!

Only she wasn't Miss Eleanor anymore. She was Mrs. Edwards! Mrs. John Edwards!

Papa married Miss Eleanor, not Mrs. MacKay!

She looked very happy and said Papa was a re-markable man, which made him wink and look ex-tremely pleased with himself.

Papa took my prospecting clothes back to the store and bought some for Miss Eleanor. She wore a heavy divided skirt and laced boots, a man's shirt, and a big hat and had her flannel nightie rolled up in her bedroll so as to save room on the burro when they went prospecting. Papa put his arm around her and said they'd get her a horse.

When Miss Eleanor married Papa, she came into her inheritance, and she gave it to Papa to finish off the grubstake.

"But, Miss Eleanor, you may lose all your money!" I said, though not where Papa could hear, as he might have gotten his feelings hurt.

"I can always *earn* more," she said.

"How?" I asked.

"Baking pies," she said, and I expect she can.

Mrs. Wheeler said she didn't know what she was going to do without Miss Eleanor. The boarders had gotten spoiled with her good cooking. She said the least Papa could do was to find her another cook. And while he was at it to find her a handyman to put in the electric for her.

"Oh!" I said.

Everybody looked at me, and Papa asked what brilliant idea had popped into my head.

"Aunt Eunice can cook," I said. "And Uncle George is real good at fixing things."

"Write 'em!" said Mrs. Wheeler. "It's worth a try." So I did.

Mrs. Wheeler and the Bentons (including Buster) came to the wedding. The preacher looked a little surprised, but he did up the job anyway. He looked surprised because Miss Eleanor wore her divided skirt and boy's boots. After the ceremony we all went to Mrs. Wheeler's for wedding cake.

Buster swiped the first piece and stuffed it down his mouth. Then he fished the strawberries out of the punch bowl and ate them. And when we all trooped down to the train station, he got stuck in a trash can. The station attendant had to grease his head to pull him out.

The Colonel had stopped calling him a "lively little

fellow" after Buster shot him in the you-know-where. Now he calls him "that young rapscallion" and says he won't be surprised if Buster ends up one of those fellows who go over Niagara Falls in a barrel.

As the train pulled out, Papa and the Colonel waved their hats at us. Miss Eleanor just waved, and Charlie had a grin wide enough to split his face. Papa didn't look much older than Joel. In my head I could just hear Aunt Eunice sniff and say, "Off on another wild-goose chase!"

"Papa won't ever change," said Joel.

"No," said Damaris.

"But that doesn't mean he doesn't care about us!" I said.

"I like your papa," said Rose, waving back at Papa as the engine hooted again.

I hugged her and said, "So do I!"

It doesn't really matter anymore that Papa is not what you call a Proper Papa. I expect he does do the best he can.

And we're used to doing without any papa at all. Damaris and Joel and I, we know how to take care of our own selves. That's what Mama taught us to do, so we don't really need him anymore, though I wouldn't tell him that, because it might hurt his feelings.

Philippa looked over her glasses at the train and asked in a very loud whisper, "What are you going to call Miss Eleanor now that she's your stepmother?"

"I don't know," I said slowly.

It felt very peculiar for Miss Eleanor to be my step-mother, but I guessed I would get used to it.

"I'm so glad you're coming with us, Abby," Rose said. "We can learn the hula dance, and you can write about Amaryllis the Fairy Child in the Sandwich Islands!"

"It's the Hawaiian Islands," Philippa said.

I nodded absentmindedly. I was thinking about Miss Eleanor and how I didn't really mind her being my stepmother, though probably Mrs. MacKay would have been all right too.

"What do hula girls wear under their grass skirts, Abby?" Philippa asked, bringing me back to earth with a great thunk.

"I don't know," I said, watching Buster twirl around at the end of his leash.

"I expect Buster will find out," said Rose.

"Ess!" said Buster cheerfully.